Dying Behaviour of Cats

Dying Behaviour of Cats

Marc Labriola

QUATTRO BOOKS

The publication of DYING BEHAVIOUR OF CATS has been generously supported by the Canada Council for the Arts and the Ontario Arts Council.

 Canada Council   Conseil des arts
for the Arts   du Canada

 ONTARIO ARTS COUNCIL
CONSEIL DES ARTS DE L'ONTARIO
an Ontario government agency
un organisme du gouvernement de l'Ontario

Cover painting: Elisabeth Labriola
Cover design & typography: Jared Shapiro
Editor: Luciano Iacobelli

Library and Archives Canada Cataloguing in Publication

Labriola, Marc, author
    Dying behaviour of cats / Marc Labriola.

ISBN 978-1-988254-44-9 (softcover)

    I. Title.

PS8623.A3329D95 2017   C813'.6   C2017-905714-6

Published by Quattro Books Inc.
Toronto, Canada
www.quattrobooks.ca

Printed in Canada

For Veronica

Day One

ONE

Theo ashed his cigarette on the egg-shaped photograph of a woman. He took a shot out of a red votive candle holder. He knew how many would take him from laughter to confession. Euphoria always ends with puking your guts out. He shot another one. Theo gagged. Last time he tried it in the downstairs bathtub he couldn't get past the depression of his breathing. Tonight he was going for the grand mal. He pictured how his body would look. Writhing like a wounded stag. Then a coma. No arousal to pain. Theo was down to one last smoke. Two more eggs in the fridge. He listened to the last sax growl on Coltrane's "Saturn" and staggered downstairs. There were two uses for the basement bathtub. Theo looked in the bathroom mirror and jabbed his thumb between his eye and his nose. He reached round and grabbed the muscle in his neck. Twisted. Then he pressed his fist hard into his sternum. Theo could still feel.

Tomorrow she'd find him. Surely tomorrow. She'd come home. Find him naked and drunk tomorrow. But Theo knew he would never be found. He would drown. Bloat. Melt into the tub. Theo knew exactly how many days it would take for his body to become part of the house. He was an expert on decomposition. Best-case scenario, he'd be found because of his smell.

He wanted to drink enough to still be drunk even though he was dead. Belligerent in the afterlife. Theo thought I hope I swallow this fucking tongue. He put down the votive glass on the lip of the tub and turned on cold. Then hot. He felt with the back of his hand for the right temperature for drowning. He kept the taps on and stopped up the drain. Climbed in. Theo lay back in the tub and waited for the smell of orange blossoms that isn't really there. He always smelled flowers right before. Theo's vocal chords seized and he screamed. He felt the water rise. Felt his balls become buoyant. Like two eggs floating in a bowl.

Two

Theo didn't know about the riot. He thought it was a parade when he saw the cow float in the street. Then tear-gas rounds came through the front window and the gas filled the house. He didn't know about the extreme weather events going on around the world. He didn't know about the garbage strike that lasted two months. Didn't know about the drunk that was killed right outside for pocket change. Two guys kicking the laughs out of him. Didn't know about the whore swallowing in the alley and falling asleep in the fetal position on the front stoop. Theo knew nothing about outside.

His dad's house was one of the last houses on the street. The others were smashed down. Up went low-rise housing projects. A men's shelter. Methadone clinic. A slaughterhouse and a couple meat-packing plants. Theo's dad would never sell. He lost his finger building the roof. Now the whores came and went like migratory birds on the sidewalk. The homeless flying their signs. Over the years Theo saw signs that read sex for food. Punch me in the face for $2. Pregnant and hungry. No God or money. $1 to watch me starve.

He didn't know about any of this for the same reason he had to hear about the newborn hurricane slowly moving up from Mexico in the nightly news. He wouldn't have even realized it was pouring cats and dogs if he hadn't felt rain in his wrist from what happened when he was 17. He didn't know about the hurricane because he hadn't left the house in seven years.

At the end of a great love, Theo thought, you amass a number of words which can break your heart in an instant. For Theo they were words like red and egg and *agua mala*. Sounds and songs and objects become tragic like things loved by the dead. It was the name of the storm that broke Theo's heart. It started out as just a tropical depression. It could have grown into Licinia, Rhea, Silvia, Sabina, Bellona, Aelia. Any other tropical cyclone woman's name. No. It had to be Catalina. Hurricane Catalina. Coming up from Mexico. Cat. Theo felt the memory of the breath of her laugh on his neck as he put his head deeper under water.

The glass of the basement window smashed. Water came rushing in the window high up on the wall. Shit street water. Right into Theo's tub. The bathroom was flooding full of newspapers and coffee cups, a beer can, eggshells. Human garbage. A dead bird came in. Brown and ugly. Female. Theo started frantically shovelling water from the tub with his hands like a sinking ship. He couldn't keep up. The water kept rising. What the fuck is happening? Where's it coming from? Theo thought the sewer pipes burst and all the city shit was drowning him. The water wouldn't stop. He tried to get up but he slipped under. Cracked the back of his head off the porcelain lip. The posterior fontanelle. The part you never touch on a baby. All that water was fucking up his drowning. He coughed out a woman's name. Theo grabbed hold of the sides of the tub and stood up. He felt his body regain its weight. He kicked his way to the door. Water still pouring through the window.

Theo staggered up to his attic bedroom. Took the stairs on all fours. Shivering and hiccupping like a newborn. Half-blind from the water of Catalina. Theo looked out the window. Black water was grovelling against the house. The street was flooded. He looked up into the night sky. Theo felt a dizzy spell. Felt the blood rush towards his heart. His arms went numb. Legs numb. Cock and balls numb. He was going to pass out. He caught himself and knelt down. With his chin on the windowsill, he took one last look for Uranus and 4 Vesta with his naked eye. It was just the right time of year to see them. His attic window looked out onto the roof of the house. In the dark he watched as an animal leapt from the branches of the tree onto his roof. It was a leopard.

Theo lay face-down on the floor. Staring at his dead dad's alto sax under the bed. So tonight it was leopards. He hallucinated animals before. Sometimes mating calls from the pictures of Catalina. But mostly voices from his dad's instruments. The leftover instruments from his nights playing sax for the Bones of Adam. Theo swore he heard a growl outside. He raised his body to the window and passed out cold. Hit his left eye off the windowsill.

THREE

When Theo was a little kid going through the sleepless years he came to his dad's bedroom. Theo knew even as a little kid what his dad didn't have the heart to say. Mothers tell bedtime stories. His dad only knew two stories for little boys. One of them was the story of the shipwreck. But he wouldn't tell his son that story for another two decades, shitting himself, hallucinating, and smelling posthumous roses in his deathbed. The other story, the one he did tell on the sleepless nights, was the story about the animals. They sat on the floor and his dad opened up all his instrument cases. The bird in the story was played by the jazz flute. The elephant was the double bass. Theo thought it looked like an elephant too. His dad made the saxophone growl for the jungle cat.

Theo would always get in trouble for touching the instruments. His dad didn't want to teach him to play. Afraid that his son would be a brilliant sax player. Being a musician is shit and you end up being a roofer anyway and getting the finger of your left hand cut off in an accident. The only thing you learn is catcalls. His dad could barely play anymore. What he did teach Theo, on one of the bad nights, was how to growl on the sax.

First his dad taught him to play one steady note. He got it. Now I want you to do exactly as I tell you. I want you to scream into the mouthpiece, Theo. The mouth is more important than the fingers. Nothing came out. He tried it again. Nothing. Theo started laughing into the mouthpiece. Laughing won't work, Theo. Only screaming. Keep at it. He tried to roar. No, don't roar, Theo. Just scream. Only the sax growls. His dad let him keep the gold alto sax with the word *Jupiter* etched into it under his bed. It's hard to scream with your mouth closed, Son. But you'll learn.

Sometimes when Theo couldn't sleep or had a bad dream, he got up and sat at the foot of his bed and tried to scream into the sax. Then one night he got it. The growl. The only sound that he could get out of it was a higher pitch than when his dad did it. He woke up his dad to let him hear. That's a female growl, Theo.

FOUR

It started with a drop of blood in his father's eyeball. Dr. Magliochetti told him there was a cherry-red spot on his retina. You're bleeding into your eye. Now it's scarred. Macular degeneration, Dr. Magliochetti said. Makes everyone look like a degenerate. The two old men laughed about macular degeneration.

Theo was 31 then and wondered if scarred and bleeding eyes were hereditary. Theo had bad eyes. Sometimes he opened his eyes in the morning and there on the ceiling was a pattern of little black circles. This happened since he was a kid. He would stand up and the circles would move with him. Black circles in the mirror. At the bottom of the stairs. In the frame of the front door. Like he was always walking towards a constellation of black stars. The pattern was never the same. But there were recurring shapes. Theo often made out the upside-down Y shape of a crab. He never told his dad about the stars.

During those first nights blind his father started falling out of bed. He didn't know how to be blind. People say that when you lose your sight your other senses are heightened. Bullshit. His dad started hearing nothing. Had to turn his jazz all the way up. Said his food tasted like dog food. He started seeing things. He would wake up and see dogs in the bed. Female dogs. Bitches, he said. How do you know they're female, Dad? Grow the fuck up, Theo. The pussies.

Theo moved back in after the primates appeared in the bathroom. The baboon had perfect timing anyway. Theo had nowhere else to go after he split with Catalina and sold the house. He couldn't stand the idea of renting a bachelor. He remembered the exact day that the baboon appeared on the shitter in his dad's bathroom because that was the day Theo and Catalina sold off all the wedding gifts in their house. They had an estate sale. Like the kind you have when you're dead. Theo watched a new couple carry out his marriage bed piece by piece.

On his first night at his dad's he slept on the downstairs couch. He felt too sad to sleep in his boyhood room. His dad left it untouched like the room of a dead kid. He woke up around 3 AM to a one-sided conversation. Who the hell is Dad calling in the middle of the night? He went upstairs and his dad was sitting straight up in bed having a conversation with her. The baboon was also female. Whenever this happened he had to figure out what his father was hallucinating based on the nature of the conversation. Another time he heard, so can you fuck with that trunk? Never wake a man talking in his sleep. Later he asked his dad what you talk to a baboon about. Sex. When it got bad Theo moved a mattress into his dad's room. His father farting and screaming through the night. Sometimes his dad would wake up scared shitless and start feeling around the king bed.

The bad year started just before his dad went blind. When the colour red was lost. Theo's dad started calling red, black. Threw out all the apples. Thought he was possessed by the devil when he nicked himself shaving. So when he claimed his cock was blue, Theo thought nothing of it. Just a blue cock. Ended up full penectomy within six months. Blindness and dick cancer. Men's diseases, his dad said when he lost his sight.

Theo slept in the hospital with his dad the night before the amputation. There was an area of Sacred Heart for the pre-op patients. That night it was only men. There were a few wives in the afternoon, but they all went home. There were six men in his dad's ward. At first no one spoke to each other, but by the end they were all shooting the shit. All the curtains open. It was dinnertime. The last meal before the fast. They were having their meat. Who knew they had black Jell-O? Then the apple juice. Nobody asked what pieces of themselves were going to be removed in the morning. Dr. Magliochetti checked in on his dad after the surgery. How are you feeling this morning? Like hell. OK, what are the symptoms of hell?

FIVE

When they got home his dad was changed. The wandering started. Then the face without emotion. Like a neutered dog. Theo caught his dad hiding things. Mostly junk that belonged to Theo's mom. He was told she collected things. Old espresso cups, this trumpet with bite marks, an old bottle that said anisa. His dad said that she bought old things at the Sacred Heart church bazaar. Dead people's shit, he called it. When Theo was a kid he snuck into her closet to smell her stuff. He imagined her. Spending her nights finding things. Like a cat prowling in the all-night places. The bus station, the coin laundry, the 24-hour streetcar that passed his bedroom window.

Playing in her closet, Theo pretended that every object he touched warned of seven years of something. He told his friends at school that he didn't have a mom. No, she's not dead. She left before I was born. He believed that until one of the boys took pity and told him about pussies. His dad wouldn't answer any questions about her. Like she didn't exist. But according to his dad, she wasn't dead. To prove it, his dad showed him the letters she stopped sending.

A few weeks after the dick surgery, Theo came back from work and his dad was splayed on his chair in the living room. Hunched in front of the TV. Pants around his ankles. Fist between his legs. On TV was a man sucking the milk out of a lactating woman's breasts. The next day it was menstruation porn. Real sick shit. After that there was always porn on. Soon he bored of the porn and just watched news. But he always watched with his pants down.

His father forgot the household dangers. He stuck his pinky in the electrical outlet. Burned his palm on the element bad. Refused to be taken to the hospital. Theo had to baby-proof the house. He found his dad sitting with his feet out the attic window once. At first he thought his dad was trying to kill himself, but considering that he had the mind of a nine-year-old boy, he figured his dad was trying to fly. After all, there was more than one nocturnal bird to make an appearance in the aviary of his king bed. Once, his dad went to the top shelf of Theo's mom's closet and unlocked his Remington Model 870 pump-action shotgun. Theo pawned the gun the next day. Worried that his dad would start hunting the savanna of his bedroom.

He refused to get his hair cut at Nic's like he did for the past 40 years because he said I'll go cross-eyed. He became obsessed with his own navel. He obviously wouldn't cut his fingernails at night. He started misnaming his own parts. Calling his mouth his asshole. Staying up all night looking for his ring finger in the bell of his saxophone. Where the hell did I leave that damn thing? Always falling out of bed. He woke up with bruises in strange places. The side of his nose. Or just below the lip. How'd you get that, Dad? He started claiming that certain things in the house would bruise him. The people in certain photographs. The neck of one particular bottle. The mouthpieces of certain brass instruments. Parts of the house didn't abide by the laws of gravity. He told Theo that he could levitate in his wife's closet when he breathed in hard. It smells female. If it wasn't for the damn roof, I would ascend right into heaven. At times it seemed that his father was not so much suffering from severe dementia as he was the demonic possession of a lovesick old man.

His dad was living in different years at once. Theo couldn't tell if it was a few years behind or a few years ahead. In any case, it wasn't now. His dad's stuff had a life of its own. It would strangely reappear at different places and in different years like a junkie wife. The leather suitcase with the Paris sticker went missing Christmas Eve 2007 two years before he died, then turned up on September 20, 2008, packed, sitting by the front door. The portable record player went missing the first of June when Theo came to stay, and reappeared playing Miles' "Blue in Green" at 4AM in January. Then it was finally lost forever that November. A woman's wide-brimmed wool fedora would appear and disappear, usually Fridays. The turquoise Underwood typewriter with keys that make kissing sounds went missing from his bedroom. Found again one year later, out of ribbon. The cat would turn up every three months. Theo thought that his dad was somehow connected to the fate of the things his wife left behind.

One night Theo came home from the construction site and there was his dad, just lying in his bed as if it weren't burning. Cigarette still smoking on his pillow. And him just lying there chewing on the ends of his laugh. It made Theo laugh when his dad locked himself up in the toilet yelling at his own empty crotch. Come on, wake up you motherfucker. Raving in there. As if he had to use up every scrap of sound he ever heard in his whole sorry life. Lullabies. Eulogies. Scatting. Baboon mating calls. Growling saxophones. He blacked out at certain songs. One of them was Coltrane's "Saturn." Most of the songs on the B side of the *Interstellar Space* album. Or "The Night Has a Thousand Eyes." One really weird thing was that he played his records backwards. Theo would find him on the middle of the bedroom floor cross-legged. Just got done levitating, Theo.

At night he wouldn't sleep. It's hotter than a six-peckered cat in here. The seasons changed in the bedroom. He stammered around the house. Get back to bed, Dad. What are you doing down here? He was separating objects. All objects come in two kinds. Male or female. You couldn't get to sleep during those male female nights. Bedroom curtains were female. Lightbulbs female. Most fruits were female except the obvious male ones. His camera was male. Bottles of bourbon. Closets were female. The roof was male. Other things were neuter. He separated the stuff into different rooms. He didn't want any fornication amongst the objects in his house. He could only dream if he fell asleep in the female half of the house.

He believed that household objects were cursed parts of the human body. Stove burners were the whorl of condemned giant fingerprints. His coat in the closet was the torso of a great hanged dictator. His musical instruments were animals or severed sex organs. His guitar was a woman's torso. Why am I living with this headless woman?

Theo understood the thing about the instruments. He felt that one day he'd be crazy like that too. When he was a kid and his dad was out of the house, Theo didn't play the instruments. He played with them. Anyway, the only thing he knew how to play was that stupid female growl. He stopped seeing them as instruments, but beasts in repose. Sea creatures. Curled up serpents. Half man, half animal. Extinct prehistoric beasts with long necks, claws, engorged phalluses. Or the bones of decomposing animals with twisted vertebrae.

Pass me the uterus, his dad said at breakfast. Fruit were usually the insides of women. An avocado was a uterus. The grapefruit, cut open, were the glands of a woman's tits. The hell he knew about glands of a woman's tits, Theo never knew. Olives were ovaries. He became convinced that he was living inside of a woman's fertile body. One time around Christmas, Theo had brought some dried figs and after eating half of them his dad said, I'm turning into a fucking woman, eating so many of these dry pussies.

Six

Smell my palms, Theo. His dad was sitting on the bed with his sax and one bare foot. I smelled them when I was playing. They smell like Black-Eyed Susan. Who? It's a flower, Theo. Do you smell that? Theo smelled them. His fingers smelled of saxophone. Black-Eyed Susan, no? My sense of smell is dead-on today. His dad held his foot out. Smells like Desert Rose. This was his father's premonition of death. He was smelling the flowers that would grow out of his corpse. Sunflowers out of my bad knee. Sage out of my heart. Rose of Sharon out of the lacrimal bone of my skull. Trumpet Vine from my severed finger. Tiger Lily where my cock used to be.

On Monday he would be dead. The same day he finally told Theo about the shipwreck. Swear to God this is true. No one would've even known there was a shipwreck if it wasn't for me, his dad said. I was nine, Theo. I kept telling my dad that the fish washing up on shore were saxophones. Theo's dad grew up in a tiny coastal town that no one ever heard of. My dad told me to fuck off and go play blocks. There I was. This little nine-year-old boy. Singing Christmas songs with dirty words to stave off the tears. I went down to the shore and brought this thing into the house and put it right there on the kitchen table. I was singing peace on earth and mercy mild, goddam sinners wreck a child. Mom screamed. It looked like a giant seahorse covered in underwater garbage. Dad wiped it off with the classifieds. I stuck my hand right inside of it, Theo. I pulled out a fistful of Lucifer prawns, and sea lavender, and little hermit crabs, and sea stars. The three of us got it wiped off. And there on the kitchen table was a gold alto sax. Swear to God. We all examined it. I found something. The word *Jupiter* was etched into it. My dad wrapped the sax in the Sunday paper and took me and the sax down to the shore. There, floating on the waves were flutes, piccolos, clarinets, every kind of saxophone. There was a beached tuba. A couple of stranded trombones. My dad told me to pick a piccolo to take home with me. He was going to hurl the sax back in the sea. But I begged for this sax.

My father tried to think, he told Theo. Which authority do you call in the case of a natural disaster of woodwinds and brass? The lady on the other end thought he was crazy. The local drunk. Finally he was connected with the Receiver of Wreck. First time I heard the name, I thought the ship was a woman. *The Norea*. She was missing. Headed here from Taiwan or some place. Carrying forks and knives and spoons and more than 500 musical instruments.

Every night after it happened, Theo's nine-year-old dad watched the news of the shipwreck. Watched the divers. Watched as death was declared in absentia for the 33 men on board. Interviews with the widows. Then seven days later, the discovery. The overturned ship with the captain collapsed on the huge hull. Near dead. *Norea* had flipped upside down. They couldn't figure out how it happened. There were experts. Conspiracy theories. But Captain Cole Day had lived. The image of Captain Day raising his head off the hull of the upside-down ship was all over the news. In all the papers.

The captain was hero-worshipped when they found him. A real man. But three days later, another body was discovered. It wasn't the body of one of the 32 other crew members. And it wasn't found by the rescue crews or the coast guard. It was me who found her, Theo. A woman doing the deadman's float. First time I saw a dead body. Nothing on her body could identify her. They checked the ship's departure documents. There was no evidence of a woman on the ship. She wasn't on *Norea*'s manifest. Later they found out that she was smuggled on by Captain Day. No one ever found out who she was.

Seven

It was Sunday. Theo woke up on his mattress on the floor. His father was missing. He went down to the main floor expecting his father fetal under the stairs. He tried to think. Where does a blind old man nine-year-old go? Theo thought like a boy. Under the bed. The table. The trunk. It ended up a 13-hour search, including Sacred Heart Emergency. When Theo found him, he went back to his father's attic bedroom. Theo sat down on his father's bed. Turned the TV on. Beside the TV was the window. He got up, opened the curtains, and looked out. His father was sleeping quietly on the roof. Theo should have known. Thirty years as a roofer.

Day Two

ONE

Theo woke up. There was a constellation of black stars on the ceiling. The crab. He sat up. Felt the goose egg at the back of his head. His eye was killing him. He didn't have to look to know it was black. He reeked of piss. He needed a smoke but was out. The lightbulb on the bedroom ceiling was dripping. He got off the floor and went to the bathroom. It looked like a single, perfect black rose petal under his left eye.

Theo stood naked at the top of the stairs. Looked at his huge reflection in the water on the main floor. He went down and kicked through to the kitchen. There was shit everywhere. Like the flood returned to him everything that he lost over the last seven years. Theo was rigged for catastrophe. This half-cocked apocalypse didn't faze him. Theo tried the stove. The wall sparked. He opened the fridge. Took out one of his last two eggs. He put the egg on his eye. Theo poured out coffee from another time. He was used to that bitter shit. He needed it. Theo wanted to warm it up with some booze, but he was out. He needed to stave the shakes off. How many days until the latest end of the world would be over?

He put the egg down and went to the garage. He had to force the door. Theo pulled down the generator from the wooden shelf. Then a can of old gas. He hauled them up the stairs one piece at a time counting down 12 hours on an 8-gallon tank. Two cans left. That's three days of light. Theo set down the generator in the bedroom at the back of the house. Uncoiled the orange extension cord that was snaked round. He filled the tank praying over that old gas. Set the thing full choke. Three tugs at the starter and it came to life. He opened up the sliding door and shoved it onto the balcony without pulling back the curtain. He left the door open a crack and snaked the cord down the hall into his dad's room and plugged in the TV and the bedside lamp.

Theo figured he better check on the world. He couldn't see out because all the windows on the main floor were boarded up by the city after the Day of Blood riot. They figured the house was condemned. Theo stuck his head out the window of the attic bedroom. The sky was spitting. It felt good. Felt good to be not dead. He looked around. The little three-storey down the street was wrecked. Like someone unbuilt it. All the pieces were just floating there in the water. The electrical poles cocked like the masts of half-sunk ships. Hell and high water, Theo thought. The pitched roofs of the last remaining houses in his neighbourhood were nearly all torn off. They couldn't withstand the uplift of wind. His dad's house, with the gable and the catslide roof at the back, stood strong. The flat roofs held out. Theo peered into the top floor of his neighbour's place. Like a doll's house. The bedroom was destroyed. The sheets of the queen were strewn around the room. Toppled drawer. Spilled panties. The end of the world is perfect for perverts.

The only damage done to his father's room was that the framed poster of his jazz band, with the name Bones of Adam in bold letters, fell from above the bed. Theo watched the street. This young couple passed in a boat singing some drunk song. A taxi was floating down the street with its emergency lights going. He wanted to check his own roof for a cave-in. Then he realized he was naked. Inside the house he wasn't naked. He went to his father's closet and grabbed some of the dead man's clothes. He couldn't find any socks. He hadn't worn shoes in probably four years. He climbed up on the windowsill and swung his feet outside. Then he turned around. Got up on his knees and stood up on the sill. He held on to the lip of the attic roof and peered over the edge. Straddling the hips of the roof was a leopard.

There's a leopard on my roof. Theo went back inside. Delirious. He needed to get back on the booze before everything started doubling as something else. He didn't want pink elephants coming from his dad's double bass. A zoo full of animals would come out of all the instruments in the house if he let it get that far. Theo had to remember that everything was ass-backwards now. You're sober when you drink, drunk when you're sober. Being a drunk is hard.

He went back to his boyhood room. He slept in his father's bed now, but his room, the one at the end of the upper floor was untouched since he moved out to become an architecture dropout. On his bookshelf he still had his book of mythology, a set of children's illustrated encyclopaedias, and a name your baby book. He took three encyclopaedias off the shelf. The C, the J, and the L. They were still in the alphabetical order of an obsessive nine-year-old. It occurred to him that he didn't know what a leopard was. How should he know? He sat down at his kid desk. Inside the cover of the book was a folded magazine clipping that he cut out when he was a boy. A cave painting of Venus and the Sorcerer. Theo flipped to Jaguar. After a few minutes he got it down to Cheetah or Leopard. Cheetah — black lines from the centre of its eyes running down to its mouth like black tears. Leopard — gold with rose patterns on its fur.

He knew the delirium was still kicking. He went back to the attic room to check if his hallucination was where he left it. Black rose patterns or black tears? He stuck his head out to the roof. At first he didn't see it. Then, from around the back of the roof, the animal walked into view. Its fur was wet. Colour of brass. Theo watched as it began to edge around the roof. He tried to catch its eye. It raised its head. No black tears. His cat wasn't crying. It was a leopard then, according to any nine-year-old boy. Theo felt all right about his leopard. He walked around his dad's room following the sound of the leopard's footsteps. He prowled around like that for a while, waiting out the withdrawal.

Theo sat down on the floor in front of the record player and dropped the needle on John Coltrane's "Catwalk." Then he played "Violets for Your Furs." Coltrane version. He pulled the record off. Picked up the spool of red thread and the pencil stub. He put the spool on the spindle of the turntable. Put Coltrane face-down and stuck the lead end of the stub through the record hole and into the spool. The record looked like it was levitating. This was his dad's little transcendental dementia trick for music. He screwed off the stylus and screwed it back on upside down. Then he loosened the counterweight at the far end of the arm as far back as it would go. Lifted the stylus to the underside of the record and let her spin. "Come Rain or Come Shine" played backwards. At the end of his days, his dad sat listening for half the night looking for divine messages in Charlie Parker's *Bird is Free*. Theo would wake when he heard the heartbeat sound at the end of the record. His father slumped in the chair. Exhausted from outrunning the black magic of his jazz. Theo sat there listening as "Violets" began from the end.

He got up to check if his hallucinations were still real. He lifted the window and looked down. The water had been slowly moving backwards into the group. Theo was a little disappointed. He was keeping his fingers crossed for the end of the world. But by this time the water started to find all the broken shitty little cracks and holes in the city to creep in.

There was a crowd of about 12 people on the roof of one of the four-storeys across the street. All women. Theo pulled his head back in and cracked it off the bottom of the window. The posterior fontanelle. Don't go, a lady yelled. It was the first time in a long time that he'd been seen. It was strange. He got a panic erection. Hey, there's a cheetah on your roof. And in what would be the first words he'd spoken to a stranger in many years, Theo called back. He's a leopard. Theo shut the window. He felt his own blood moving backwards through his body. His dick was throbbing. He went back to the window on his knees. Peeped out. Another few people came out onto the roof. They were all pointing at Theo's father's house. The leopard was real.

He wished he still had his dad's Remington Model 870 pump-action shotgun. Theo wished he could take the gun out of his mom's closet where his dad hid it and fire a warning shot and watch them scatter. Maybe they'd jump off the rooftop and into the water. He hadn't fired the thing since he was a kid. When his dad taught him to contemplate blood.

Theo knew how to bloodtrail a stag. His dad could barely play music anymore, but he could still fire a gun. It takes fewer fingers. When you wound a stag, his dad said, and it runs off to hide, you got to track him down. You got to look for blood or you'll lose him. Blood fizzling pink on the ground is lung blood. Crimson is a heart shot. Gut shot has got bits of shit and green. Liver hit is dark. Then there's the meat hit. Theo remembered his first shot. The stag took off. His dad sent him to check the blood. Barely any blood on the leaves. Almost nothing at all. But he was sure that he hit it. He saw the stag shudder. His dad started laughing his ass off. I missed him, I missed him. No, you hit him alright, Theo. You shot his balls right off.

That's when he learned that there's barely any blood when you shoot the stag right in the genitals or ass. Theo's dad knew all about blood. But he didn't need the blood to know where he hit the stag. He knew how the male was wounded just by the way it ran and hid. Six or seven of his dad's friends would go hunting. The joke was that all of them got together when their wives were on the rag. They couldn't fuck so they went hunting.

Someone started pounding Theo's door. It scared the piss out of him. He went into the washroom to hide. There was pounding on the door again. Then the pounding stopped. He rolled his pants to the knee, and went downstairs.

Theo looked out the cracks in the plywood covering his front window. The water was up past the stairs. There were cops at the door with the water to their knees banging on the wood with a blackjack. That's when he heard it. The growl. The cops backed up and looked up at the leopard. Theo waded through the water on the main floor to the bottom of the stairs. Listened to the sound of the leopard. Spitting and snarling. There's a leopard on my roof. The blackjack banged the door again.

He climbed back up the stairs and looked out the attic window. The crowd was getting bigger. There were people on other rooftops. Some old people brought out folding chairs. A portable radio. Catastrophes make people nice. Firefighters and rescue workers showed up in these little red boats. Ones they keep for apocalypses like these. Then he heard the voice. It lingered in the air like listening to the sound of your own laugh after you've stopped laughing. We can see you in there. The firefighter was holding one of those speaking trumpets to his lips. He called out to Theo in the voice of some electric god. Open the door or we'll break it down. There's a tiger on your roof. Fuck off fireman. It's a leopard.

Then Theo saw the TV camera. He recognized Cindy. He used to jerk off to the eleven o'clock news. They were setting up on the roof across the street. He turned on the TV in the bedroom. Flipped through commercials. There it was. Theo's house was live. He almost didn't recognize the place. He never saw the outside all boarded up. He was looking at his own window backwards. It was humiliating. Someone had spray-painted a huge cock and balls on the plywood. God knows how long that cock had been there. He moved toward the window without taking his eyes off the screen. He put one open hand in the window in front of the curtain and watched it emerge on TV. That's my hand, he thought. He changed the channel. His hand was on. The scrolling caption read Leopard On Roof. Man Barricaded Inside House. He changed again. Cindy was pointing to different parts of the house. There's at least one person alive inside. At this point we are unsure whether the hand we saw belongs to a man or a woman. He thought about drooping his cock out the window. Then they showed his leopard. It was walking the edge of the roof.

Theo got up and made sure the curtain was closed tight, then watched the screen trying to track the leopard from beneath. He listened for the sound of claws on the roof. Like he used to listen beneath the songs on his dad's records for the sounds of the musicians' fingers on the saxophone keys. The leopard on his house on TV went to the back edge of the roof. Just stood there. What are you doing, leopard?

A female voice was talking about the zoo. Twenty-six animals escaped. The rhino has been captured on the onramp to the eastbound highway. The elephant was captured in the fountain by City Hall. Seven wolves were shot in the early hours. Local children have spotted a giraffe in an alleyway. Only one baboon is still unaccounted for. A female. Maybe the baboon was on Catalina's roof, Theo thought.

He flipped channels to check his roof from another angle. The alley around the back. The guy was talking about his leopard. It was male. Theo knew it. It was a Persian leopard. There was even a back story. A real sad story about the leopard. He was captured wandering around a mountain range in Turkey. Around the top of the mountain. He had no family. They didn't say anything about who found him or how they caged him or how he got to be at a zoo on the other side of the world. If the zoo hadn't take him, the anchor said, he'd have been killed for medicine or decoration.

Theo thought maybe he should open up the window and let the leopard in. Maybe the leopard would want to get drunk with him. He could sleep in his dad's bed. He could wash him in the downstairs tub. The leopard had a name too said the news. Deniz. It was Turkish. Sounds like a girl's name. Deniz the leopard. The reporter was interviewing Deniz' trainer in the studio. He said that the name in Turkish means sea.

Theo watched for the next hour until the six o'clock news. The hour when you find out all the ways the world is going to hell that day. There on TV was his house. His hand waving. His leopard that means sea. Theo flipped channels. The news was on in Spanish, in Chinese, it's in fucking Urdu. It was the top story. This was international news. Theo's house. Theo's leopard. Theo's hand was the face of Hurricane Catalina. The face of the end of the world.

Deniz was the lead story. He bumped the story of the girl who was held captive for eleven years in the basement of a house not twenty minutes from him. Bumped the severed heads hanging off that bridge in Mexico. Bumped the surgery of the male conjoined twins. Bumped the executing of students in the protest south of the border, the kidnapped girls, the suicide bombing. Bumped the massacre in the restaurant that Theo was following every night. The wacko who made all the diners keep eating then shot them to shit. Bumped the extreme weather events around the world. Bumped the news of the food shortages. The riots in every major city. There was more coverage than the meat riots on the Day of Blood.

Two

Electromagnetic radiation was flickering across the sky. Invisible wavelengths were bouncing off the wind. And all this celestial data lead to one conclusion: Catalina. They interrupted coverage of his leopard to give the forecast. The end of the world was measured in centimetres. Record rainfall hit the city last night.

He flipped around the channels looking for himself. Terrified that he might hear the words shut-in. Recluse. Hermit. Pervert. One network zoomed in on his hand. They called in a hand surgeon. She declared him a man. At least he had that. The one who cuts it off knows it best, Theo figured. He changed the channel again and right then and there, on the six o'clock news, Theo was revealed to the world. They had a photograph of him. Looking out the attic window. One black eye.

Theo prayed Catalina was watching. A new female reporter was questioning the crowd keeping watch on the roof across the street. Do you know him? Have you ever seen him outside? Why doesn't he come out? Good question, bitch. Maybe because being nine and looking up women's first names that start with O in a gas station phone book. Maybe because hand-foot-and-mouth disease before his first communion. The doctor called it coxsackievirus and kids said cocksucker virus. Maybe because his father said that he could still feel his finger even though it wasn't there. Later his cock. Maybe because he still remembered getting hit in the back of the head when he was seven and all of a sudden his mouth tasted like cap gunpowder. He remembered a fight with Nick in the third grade, the punch in the side of the head tasted like putting your tongue on a 9v battery. All the other times he hit his head it tasted like street before it rains. Take your pick of small catastrophes. Maybe he didn't come out of his house because he just wanted to give the world time to forget his name. But for Theo, out of all the reasons he had to abandon the world like an unwanted newborn, the real reason was because of her disappearance from his life.

He wanted Catalina to see him this way. In pieces. Just a hand. A black eye. The drawback of withdrawing from the world is that you can never show off your pain. Theo hoped Catalina was one of the women in the crowd growing enormous on the roofs of the houses.

THREE

Theo was fucking up at work. Showing up late or drunk. Got choked up in the portable shitter once. The workers said nothing because his wife left him and his dad just died. Theo stayed on in his dad's house. He had nowhere else to go. After a shoving match with one of the older guys on the site, the foreman told him to take a walk. Two weeks paid. Get your shit together. He didn't answer his phone or door to anyone. After the fifth week, when he showed up without word at a new foundation the crew was digging, he was fired. He finished cleaning out his dad's bank account, which he had been slowly doing since the funeral. He went home. Stashed the money in an empty sax case.

This was right around the Day of Blood. There were droughts in Australia and China. Water riots. Record-high temperatures in the Mediterranean. Cold waves in South America. There were sugar riots in Cuba. Flour riots in the UK. Potato riots in Russia. There were two whisky rebellions. A beer riot. Rum riot in El Salvador. Bread riots across Europe. Champagne riot. Rice riots. Wine riots in Italy.

The meat riot started just a few blocks from Theo's house near the slaughterhouse and the meat-packing plant. The price of pork and chicken doubled in a month. Beef and lamb tripled. There were rations in the grocery store. Brawls in the meat aisle. Women hoarded lipstick and other cosmetics made from cow carcasses. Theo often wondered if Catalina was starving. He wasn't worried about her. He just couldn't picture her waiting in one of those huge meat line-ups. He pictured her slowly gathering up women. Distributing little vials of theatrical blood. Checking if the viscosity was right. Taking into account the effect of the lunar phase on a woman's uterus. Then teaching the women one by one which part of their body to paint red.

Theo could only afford beef tripe and chicken gizzard. He had been dipping into the stockpile of apocalypse soups and canned ham he kept stacked in the basement. After a round of firings at the slaughterhouse near Theo's place, the rest of the workers went on strike. On the Day of Blood, a group of workers fired on their Friday night shift after boning and cutting the animals showed up at the building. Prodded by the protesters, they crossed the picket lines and threw Molotov cocktails in fruit juice bottles through the windows of the meat-packing plant. Three of the fired men scaled the fence on the other side of the slaughterhouse. A few minutes later the three came round the front pulling a live steer.

Another crowd of protesters swarmed the animal. They paraded the steer down the street. Everyone was chanting, in the belly of the beast, we the people have to eat! Everyone grabbing at the steer. There were so many people holding on and pulling the animal in different directions that for a few seconds while he passed Theo's house, the steer had somehow been completely lifted off the ground as the crowd moved down the street. The steer panicked and made a break for it. He kicked his way out of the air and trampled a few protesters. Side-swiped a police car. Tripped over a red fire hydrant and broke his front leg. The protesters surrounded the steer, lifted him up, and carried him down the street to the government buildings.

The steer was mooing and bleeding when they laid him down. We need meat and we need water! Get these men back to the slaughter! Riot police circled round. Protesters, like cornered animals, fought back with rocks and Molotov cocktails. Cops started firing rubber bullets. A cocktail blew over the steer and lit him up. Fire and the people, up we'll rise! We will not be victimized! Theo watched the smoke from the attic window. People go crazy when they're starving. There were reports that some poor people ate their cats.

Riot police shot water cannons at the protesters. They ran off down the street. The steer was still blazing and screeching. A cop fired a round into its head. Groups of protesters hid behind buildings. One group hid out in the alley by Theo's house. When the cops rounded the corner the protesters let them have it with rocks. The riot police shot back with tear gas. A shell smashed right through Theo's front window. Tear gas filled the house room by room. Theo ran downstairs to the basement and put a wet towel under the bathroom door, like firemen tell children. His eyes were burning. He filled up the bathtub. Stuck his head under water. The rest of his windows and the front door were smashed by stray rubber bullets and stones. He hid down there in the basement bathroom weeping for seven hours. Terrified that they were going to loot his house. Drag him out and set him on fire. But no one set foot inside. By the next morning, men from the city came by and boarded up his house. They didn't say a word. Didn't even check if anyone was alive inside. They sealed up every hole except the back door. Theo never left the house again.

FOUR

Once an hour, cops or firefighters would bang on his door. They were being cautious because of the TV cameras aimed at the roof. If no one was watching, they'd just boot the door down and kick his teeth in. Piss on him. Theo didn't leave the attic bedroom. They'll have to drag me out. He stayed right there beneath Deniz. The water had receded enough that they brought in a firetruck and backed it up to the front of the house. Hoisted the ladder to the roof above Theo's window. He watched a woman come out of the back door of the truck. She wasn't a fireman. She was wearing those rubber pants and boots like his dad wore hunting sometimes. She waded up to the side of the house. She was calling the animal by his given name. She was one of those people who teach wild beasts to do carnival tricks.

The trainer went up with a bucket. Deniz must be starving. They were narrating the action on TV. Crowds on the other rooftops were going wild. The trainer was trying to establish dominance. Theo heard the footsteps of the woman on his rooftop. Get the fuck off my roof. She dumped the meat. Good meat too. Not the chicken asshole he was used to. Theo hoped Deniz would maul the trainer lady. Anyway, the ploy didn't work. Deniz didn't give two shits about the meat. Didn't even look at the lady. The TV people were more worried that the roof would cave in. Theo knew it wouldn't. What they didn't know was that his dad built the roof for live loads. Rather than the standard dead ones. It was like his dad knew that one day it would be needed to hold up a Persian leopard. And protect his shut-in boy.

At 11PM, Cindy was saying that Deniz was dangerous. At the zoo he was caged alone. It wasn't because he was born wild. It was because Deniz still had his balls. He hadn't been castrated like other big cats in the zoo. Like the male lions who lose their manes. So Deniz was ferocious. Channel 24 was giving advice about what to do if you encounter a leopard in the street. They showed an artistic rendition of a leopard in the right-hand corner of the screen like he was a flasher on the subway. Something worked up by a sketch artist from the memory of a victim. Don't walk alone at night. Don't cut through parks or wooded areas that are not well-lit. Don't let a leopard think you are an animal. Don't crouch. Look big. Don't crowd it. Don't attack it. Don't throw things at it. Don't corner it. If the leopard approaches, sing loudly.

FIVE

This reminded Theo about the incident with the cock. It must have been about five years back. Theo used to look out the window religiously. He was trying to look for Uranus with his naked eye when it happened. It wasn't the kind of man you'd suspect. No long coat. No mustache. None of the usual pervert tipoffs. He stood on the corner, leaning against the wall. Two teenage girls were passing, and he just took it out. One of the girls screamed. They both ran across the street. The other girl looked back because she didn't see anything. Just screamed because her friend did. Theo's heart beat hard. He was waiting for something to happen that is supposed to happen in these scenarios. But the guy just put it back in. Like it was the most natural thing in the world. Suppose it was. He didn't run off right away either. Just stayed there leaning on the wall. Cock back inside. Theo thought he should do something. Go out there and knock him out. Or cut his dick off. But he wasn't sure which one to do. And in the end, he did nothing. Just kept watching. A couple of squad cars passed by and Theo hid behind the curtain. They circled a couple times. Nobody got out. After the incident, Theo looked out the window for the man every day. For about three and a half years he looked for him, but he never showed.

The initial terror gave way to a bigger fear. The fear that the man would go on whipping his cock out by the corner of Theo's house. Maybe the cock was local. Then the police would be called again. Maybe the TV news would film something about the thing. Eventually police would come door to door trying to catch the stranger's cock. Asking if Theo too had seen the cock in question. Maybe he'd be interviewed on camera. What if they came to the door when he wasn't wearing pants? He never wore pants. Start wearing pants. If they did interview him on TV then Theo would be not just associated somehow with the pervert, but in the minds of the viewers, he would be the pervert himself. Forever associated, even when alone with himself, with a stranger's genitals.

Six

Theo was worried because he didn't have any food. He hadn't planned to live today. Now with the leopard and the crowds he couldn't call the grocery boy. The grocery stores were probably all flooded anyway. He pictured all the eggs just floating up and down the aisles. Frozen animal parts all thawed and soggy. The news reported looting. As a shut-in, Theo fantasized about looting. But only ever about grocery stores. Especially since the food shortage. He imagined gorging himself. Biting into bricks of cheese. Cakes. Honeyed ham. Lamb chops. Leaving a bite mark in everything.

By now Theo could teach classes on being a shut-in. Go home to home mentoring young shut-ins like a mother cat until they are ready to go out into the world and hide on their own. How do you get groceries? Easy. Call that grocery place for infirm widows. Leave cash under the mat on the steps. Use the back of the house. Only order once a month. When the meat gets too expensive, stock up on the hearts, livers, and necks of chickens. Where do you get cash from? You empty your inheritance before you go into hiding. Daily withdrawals. Keep the cash in rolls stuffed inside the instrument case in your dead dad's bedroom.

How do you keep the city from shutting off your lights? Leave a tip for the grocery guy with a note saying please mail these envelopes. He'll get the idea. What do you do in a break-in? Lie there quietly in bed until the two men leave. You'll have no idea what they stole anyway. Then be fairly sure that one of them relieved himself in the corner. Theo's survival over the last seven years was a testament to the inventiveness of solitude.

Theo tried to write. Writing is what all prisoners do. For Theo, it was mostly about suicide attempts and paid sexual encounters. They were not so different in his mind. Both escapes from the body. Theo was on a shut-in budget so he couldn't waste cash on paper. The only paper he had around was his dad's staff paper. The kind for writing music. That's where he wrote about the whores. And the dead cat.

Theo killed time. He took apart the radio like an autistic boy and put it back together again. Cut the strings off a guitar to feel the snap. Made some kids' toys out of coils from the mattress. A little truck, a scorpion, and a crab. He painted with strange colours his little figure of a saint with a padlock on his lips. He made a beautiful lamp out of a bottle of bourbon. Named the instruments after girls he wanted to kiss in grade six. Patricia and Stephanie and Amelia and Anna and Hillary Montes.

Try this if you're a shut-in. Put your ear up to the ceiling fan. Careful not to cut your head off. If you listen carefully, it sounds like an old fighter plane in the movies. Open and close your umbrella in the house. To hell with superstition. It sounds like flapping wings. Blow into your dad's brass mouthpiece and it sounds like he's not dead and instead starting up his car. Tuba or baritone work perfect. Take your grandpa's dog tag and drag the chain over the arm of the plastic lawn chair. Sounds like a snake. Whip the porcelain tub with the dog tag chain. Sounds like an electric current. Take your dad's saxophone case, close your eyes, and open up that metal latch. Gun cocking. If you tap the needle of the record player on the record it sounds like a heartbeat through a stethoscope. A woodsaw sawing sounds like a jungle cat growling. All sorts of shit sounds human. The wind sounds human. A cat in labour sounds like a woman in labour.

Theo sometimes entertained himself by observing how food rotted. He would leave a glass of milk on the table to see how long it would take to curdle. When he could still pay for it, he would observe a piece of pork. Theo left an egg out in a bowl of water to see how long it would take for the egg to turn black.

It's also entertaining to hurt yourself. Before the shortage, Theo glutted himself on food, trying to faithfully recreate Catalina's famous seared salmon, then stuck his middle finger down his throat. Retching in the kitchen sink he thought, this is good. I need to empty. Leave some room for the wrath of God. When food was scarce, he would take a gulp of bathroom cleanser. It was like some native drug vigil. The eating of sacred bark. Puking as religious experience. There was also self-burning with some of his dad's Cubans.

The booze delivery guy, before the whisky rebellion, was ripping him off. He knew about the envelope of money on the back stoop. Knew after the first time that Theo would not come out. Knew that Theo was watching him the whole time through the peephole. The booze guy made off with the cash, and the bourbon. Word got around among the delivery guys that they could rip off the cash and the bottle. So Theo tried to replace alcohol for a while. First thing he missed was the dizziness. He had a fix for dizziness. He used to do this when he was a kid. Kids love to get dizzy. Like when his dad took him to the carnival and he rode the devil's wheel six times in a row. When you spin really fast you feel like you're still, but everything around you is moving fast. Theo liked to feel like he was in orbit. Like Saturn and Uranus in his children's encyclopedia. He felt the world spinning backwards. Turning back into a kid. Back into an infant. Even further back into a fetus in his mother's belly. Into a fat little seraphim. Reversing time. After a while Theo got sick of turning into the angels.

SEVEN

Try to go as long as you can without eating. Theo went 13 days. Without sleeping. 87 hours before he started to see grey fungus on his balls. After about 90 hours he began to see parts of his body fall off. His balls rolling down the stairs. Theo chasing after them. Get the fuck back here, guys. After sleeping for two days straight, he thought that it would be fun to never speak again. The first three weeks are fun. After the sixth week, he became unspeakably hungry. Horny. Compulsively growling on the sax. Finally after seven weeks of silence, he woke up mewling.

His dream was to cut off pieces of himself to send to all the people in his life. My tongue to the whore Dalila. My dick to Catalina. No. My balls to Cat. My tongue. Who should get my tongue? My eyeballs to my mom. My ring finger to my dad for use in the afterlife. When there's almost nothing left of me I'll burn the place to the ground and they'll have to identify me by my teeth.

Theo was trying to kill himself off in small doses. There's more than one way to skin a cat, he thought. He kept track of it all on the staff paper. But the problem was that he was not dying at all. Just developing immunity to everything. Like some Turkish king of the ancient world who has animals keep watch over him as he sleeps secluded in the wild. Every day poisoning himself just a little to build a tolerance. It was only through killing himself that Theo was slowly making himself immortal.

Theo wondered about Deniz' zoo. He would like to be a trainer. But not for leopards. For snakes. There must have been snake handlers who trained themselves against the poison of the pit viper or common death adder or the other snakes with animal names in his children's encyclopedia. Rhinoceros viper. Tiger rattlesnake. There is no immunity to a leopard attack.

EIGHT

Theo couldn't hear any footsteps on the roof. Deniz didn't move for a couple hours. The helicopter showed Deniz lying perfectly still right above the attic window. Theo got scared that Deniz was dead. As long as the animal was living, he seemed to keep the people at bay. Deniz could kill any one of them. But if he was dead, this would present another problem. The cameras confirmed the rising and falling of the leopard's ribs. The trainers thought that he might have been injured by Hurricane Catalina. The cameras were zooming in on individual parts of the animal.

This reminded him of the situation with the cat. It was an Abyssinian according to his sources. He'd seen it around. He didn't know if it was a man or woman cat. In the end, he decided it was a boy. He went so far as to give him a name. Like Charlie, the mangy neighbourhood bird. Or Cannonball the raccoon. Or Sonny, the big, bearded homeless guy who sometimes slept around back. Theo called the cat Gato Barbieri. One day Gato Barbieri turned up dead in the corner of the back stoop. Cats always die in hiding. In the days before the death, Theo noticed changes in Gato Barbieri. He was bumping into things, staggering around. Acting drunk. The kid's encyclopedia confirmed it. Abyssinians have trouble with blindness. Hereditary degeneration of the retina. The staggering made Theo watch the cat all the more. It's much more interesting to watch the blind. He saw the cat lie down in the corner and not move for a long time. After half an hour Theo made some noise at the window and kicked the back door. The cat staggered off. It dawned on Theo that he interrupted a death. It is only when left in hiding that a cat is able to die. Theo too was perfecting his solitude. Living out, day to day, the dying behaviour of cats.

What Theo was most interested in was what would happen to poor old Gato Barbieri after death. He didn't want to know if cats go to heaven. He wanted to know what would happen to the cat's body. Then it happened. Based on the last time Theo looked out the window, Gato Barbieri could not have been there for more than three hours. Estimated time of death: 6AM. He was on his side, facing towards the window. His left paws were kind of stuck straight out. He wasn't neutered.

At twenty-four hours he got worried because Gato Barbieri hadn't changed at all. He thought that maybe the cat was an incorruptible. That a saintly feline had died at his home. That the pope himself would have to come verify the dead cat. But by that evening some hair fell out, and patches of the face looked blue and purple and black. Like a beaten man. By the next day, the idea of St. Barbieri was all but shot to hell. The fur kept falling out, and on the bare parts Theo noticed that the skin started to bubble as if his blood was boiling after death. Theo always imagined that his anger too would continue after death. That this is part of the nature of certain decomposing men. Theo seemed to innately understand the processes of death. He got his staff paper to make notes on the decomposition of Gato Barbieri. The kid's encyclopedia didn't say shit about decomposition. It went right from Decapitation — also known as beheading, an ancient form of execution rarely used today, and jumped right to Demeter — Goddess of fertility, daughter of Saturn, the god who mutilated his own father, Uranus.

Flies surrounded Gato Barbieri like they hatched out of his blistered skin. His first impulse was to go outside to get the flies off the cat's body. The day after that, Gato Barbieri was no longer himself. His balls were distended. Sludge was coming out of his poor blind eyes. Then his ears and mouth. Theo imagined it was coming out of all Gato Barbieri's holes. All death really is, is a change to the boundaries of the body. Two days later the cat's body couldn't hold on to its living shape. His head ruptured and separated from his neck. Then his genitals erupted and fell off.

The next time he looked, the cat's body was crawling. There were maggots coming from his eyes and mouth. In a day's time, pieces of his skin were sliding off and all his hair was falling out. It looked like his cheeks were going to burst like Dizzy Gillespie blowing on his bent trumpet. Theo was scared again when the next day the maggots left him. He thought that watching the cat interrupted the cycle of death. That week, Theo noticed that the cat's death was still alive. But it was no longer confined to his body. All the grass around him died too. This was a year before Deniz appeared on the roof.

A good slip of the kitchen knife six months ago left a three-inch long wound in Theo's left forearm. Going to the hospital was out of the question. Maybe he could make a catgut suture. In the end, Theo made the simple choice, as he had done in other matters, to do nothing. Don't waste the bourbon on another one. Don't make a tourniquet out of strips of her leftover summer dresses. Just let her go.

The first thing he noticed was that his arm became hot. After a couple nights it smelled sour. His arm was changing colour. He could feel the heat stretching up and down. It wasn't the first time that Theo considered his poisoned blood. After another night or so, an abscess formed. He hadn't imagined that. He liked it. Something new was added to him. Theo's wrist, broken on his father's chin at 17, could predict rain. Theo wondered what this new wound would predict. The abscess grew. Eventually all it did was leak. He didn't die of it. Everything just went right back to normal.

NINE

It was the only newspaper he had for a long time, so he read the news again and again for a while. All the same old catastrophes. The back pages were the whore pages. There were black bars over the girls' eyes. The eyes more private than the vagina. There were all types of females. Blonde Blonde Blonde. Wild Spanish Girl. All Real Woman. Shemale Bombshell. Red Light Special close to the airport. Latina Queen. Horny Freak. Amazon Goddess. Moroccan Beauty. Filipina Grandma. Sexy Tight Asian Doll. Smoking Remy. Pin-up-girl. Pin me down. Full menu. No holes barred. Lips and Hips. Brazilian. Daddy's Little Girl. There were women who come in twos. Chantal and Luna. Zoe and Khloe. Liya and Jazzmin. There was Puerto Rica Nika. Middle Eastern Milk and Honey. She'll take you to heaven. Endangered Exotic. Heavenly Body. Never ending pleasure. Redhead Fire Crotch. Persian Pussycat. Insatiable Angel. Grand Opening.

They were all ads to fuck a goddess. Whores are so clever. The bad puns with cum. Theo took a long time to pick his goddess. He didn't dare hail a neighborhood working girl. He called up Daddy's Little Girl. But the paper was too old and they told him she was married with a kid and doesn't do that shit anymore you fucking pervert. Some were dead probably. He called one named Dalila. A man answered. They listed the measurements of the woman. Her female statistics. Hair colour: black. Eye colour: dark brown. Bust: 36. Waist: 24. Hips: 36. Pussy: shaved.

He went with Dalila. Tell her to come round back, Theo told the man. He got himself ready for the act a few nights prior. Shave. Trim your pubes. Cut your fucking toenails Theo, it's embarrassing. There were many parts of himself he felt the need to cut off.

She'd be over in an hour. Theo watched for her from the attic window. It was 3AM and no one was out. A few cars passed and his cock got hard. He saw another car come slowly down the road. There were two people. A man was driving. The woman was pointing at the house numbers. Looking for the number where she would get out and have sex with the stranger inside. The car stopped across the street in front of his house. The woman got out. He thought of her catalogue of statistics. Her hair was black. Was her pussy shaved?

The woman walked towards the house. Theo kept looking out the window. The car wouldn't leave. She kept looking back. She probably never had sex with a man in a boarded-up house before. Theo turned on the light at the back of the house and answered the door. The first thing he remembered about Dalila was her little overnight bag. She said hi I'm Dalila what's your name? Adam, Theo said. He mumbled some excuse about the boarded-up windows. Renovating. What a joke. He brought her upstairs. His dead dad's room. She put her bag on the dresser and took out perfume, lube, hand cream. Later she would take out soap and shampoo. She knew all the things she needed to wash him off her body. She brought her own condoms to be sure he didn't pass on any disease or children. She even had a book. She told him to sit down on the bed. So you're a musician? Can you play all these instruments? No, just the saxophone. Can you play something for me? I only know one song. He opened up the sax. Theo gave her the female growl. She laughed. Dalila said, then on the Day of Atonement in the fiftieth year, blow the saxophone loud and long throughout the land. Turned out she was a very religious whore. Theo liked her right away. On another night she told him her dad was a reverend. That technically she should be burned alive. Did you know that there's only one requirement for a man to become a priest? Priests can't have damaged testicles.

Before he finally settled on Dalila as his usual girl, when Theo told her his name was Theo, he went through the whores still available through the free newspaper. He catalogued their sexual characteristics after they left on staff paper like his dad writing out his blowing changes, reliving in his head all the licks and riffs. He tried out Amazon Goddess. Counted off before orgasm. 3. 2. 1. Moroccan Beauty. Double-time grunts. Middle Eastern Milk and Honey. Lay there like a mouldy fig. Insatiable Angel. Screamed in her moving inner voice. He tried the girls in twos. Chantal and Luna. Liya and Jazzmin. Zoe and Chloe didn't work together anymore. He recorded every trill and bellow and groan and song. By the end it was written out like a jazz fake book. A bootleg guide to their genital variations. He never gave the female growl to any of them but Dalila.

The whores made him attentive to his own body. Some were old. They all came older than their picture. Some were stunning. And very expensive. He became addicted. Over the years he had been with Dalila over 100 times. You fuck me more than my own boyfriend. Theo learned that the boyfriend was the guy who waited in the car. A nice enough guy named Ted. Never roughed her up. What does he do in there? Probably jerks off, she said. Or calls a hooker.

Sometimes they wouldn't have sex. Theo would ask her to cut his hair or teach him how to make lasagne. She brought him black-market booze and canned meat when the shortage began. I wish I could quit you, Theo told Dalila after he had been calling her for the first year. OK Theo, just pay me to cut your balls off, Dalila said. She told him that she would do it for him for $1000. A man can live without balls. It's safer, she told him. When it comes time for the sacrifices, you will be excluded. Dalila was reading Leviticus again. Her favourite. Lots of talk about prostitutes. She liked the rules about semen.

Only the castrated animals are saved from sacrifice, she told him. Theo thought of his balls.

The whores devoured his inheritance. He spent the better part of a decade in and out of the whores in the paper. After a while, it wasn't even exciting anymore because sex was guaranteed. Because they already had sex, it was as if Dalila's body already included his within it. Theo existed within the repertoire of Dalila's waist. Somehow, part of himself, when she was away from him, remained submerged in her. This also disgusted him, as he knew that parts of hundreds of men remained in her as well. He turned to Dalila afterwards. What is the most common desire that men have? They all want to come inside me. That or watch me piss. Theo hadn't seen Dalila for about a year. His dad's cash was running low. In the end he chose meat over pussy.

While Dalila was on top of him on that first night, he stared hard. Not because it was years since he was with a woman, but because he was remembering how he stared at Catalina. He used to stare at Catalina for a long time. Across café tables. Across beds. After a while, if he stared long enough, he started to see her different. The little cleft in her chin. The small crease between her eyebrows. He looked for new parts of her. Eventually she looked like a new woman. A stranger. It's like saying a word again and again until it means nothing and you laugh. Catalina. Catalina. Catalina. She would laugh at him and tell him to quit that new woman thing, it makes me jealous. Theo became addicted to this game, looking forward to new parts of his wife.

After Cat, it was always nights that were worst. Jealousy is a night feeling. Catalina with another man. He didn't weep over the small things anymore. Coming across her night cream. The one for her eyes. Her rosewater. The one for her feet. Her little pink box of menstrual pads under the sink. Those little trinkets that all tragedies have. He was jealous about her body. When he thought about another man inside her. Male jealousy is only ever really about pussy.

TEN

Deniz was 12 when he was captured. Family never found. Leopards only stay with their mothers for two years before striking out on their own. Theo assumed Deniz was young and potent. All leopards are young. Deniz was not. Deniz was an old man. Leopards usually live up to 17 years. Deniz was 21. There was a good chance he would die of old age up there. TV said that in captivity, leopards live unnaturally long. Theo looked at himself in the reflection of the screen. He looked like he aged in cat years. He knew about cat years from his dad's cat.

When a cat is one, you are celebrating its 15th birthday. In the second year they've slowed down the aging. This time they only age 10 years. On the second birthday the cat's 25. After that, they slow it down again. They live four years a year. So, if by the time Theo was 2 he was 25, and then he had lived 37 more years, then 37 x 4 = 148. 148 + 25 = 173. If he doubled his age and lived to 78, then he would have made it to 346 in cat years. Like some Biblical father. He checked the Bible Dalila gave him. Abraham lived to 175. But Adam lived to 930. Noah lived to 950. Even Noah's son Shem lived to 600. Theo couldn't remember if it was that son or the other son who saw his father naked and castrated him. After the great flood, the Biblical patriarchs die off much quicker.

Theo wanted to live in cat years. He didn't have the balls to kill himself. He tried to find a way to accelerate aging. If you sped up time, would you age faster? Like turning the clock ahead one minute a day. No one would notice. He thought, if I can just gain a minute a day, in two months I'd have sped up time by one hour. Six hours a year. Then he could up his timeline. Gain five minutes a day. 5 minutes/day x 12 days = 1 hour. Every 288 days he would gain a day. Goddamn it. That's not enough. He thought he could live two days in one day. Then try for three. Move tomorrow morning's shit up to today. Get fat. Fatter. Get drunk. Have sex with two girls at the same time. Tomorrow's cry tonight.

He wanted to start everything at the end. He grabbed the Bible from beside the bed. Flipped to the last page. He wanted to see how it would all end. He who testifies to these things says, "Yes, I am coming soon." Amen. Come, Lord Jesus. The grace of the Lord Jesus be with God's people. Amen. So that was it. He went to his boyhood room and sat down on the floor. Last name in the baby name book: Zachariah. Gender: M. Remembered by Jehovah. Last entry in the children's encyclopedia: Zeus. King of the gods. Also known as Jupiter. He ripped open the box that said Catalina's books. The box he took as bait. Theo read the last lines of her anthropology books. The big ones. The ones about things hidden since the foundation of the world. He overturned the box of books on the floor. Poems of Federico García Lorca. *The Poetic Edda*. *Solomon and Saturn*. *De Medicina* by Aulus Cornelius Celsus. *Oedipus Rex*. He knew that one from his book of myths. Then *Lysistrata*. He grabbed a book and ripped out the last page. Theo read aloud the last stanzas in Cat's favourite poem by Catullus.

And sterile I must live on this cold mountain and like all others in snow-bound Ida's province, follow the deer and wild boar – a man undone, longing for home again. And as these words flowed from her glowing lips a prayer rose to the gods, Cybele released her lions, driving one nearest to her side into the forest saying: Go follow him, he who is mad Attis, mangle his brain within your claws, go follow him who longs to leave my empire; give your rage to him, transmute your madness to his person, lash tail and throw your rolling head, mane erect in fury, follow him. At this the creature sprang through the deep wilderness, and on a glittering sunstruck beach found Attis, drove him back to Ida where now wandering forever, Attis, delirious, sings praise, a servant to the goddess Cybele. Great goddess, spare me, never haunt my home – take others for your slaves, those creatures that you have driven mad and those who in their madness wake again your passionate cruelty.

Eleven

Theo moved back home to help his father speed along his own death. Soon his dad died. Theo's own withdrawal from the world began with the cuffs on his father's suit pants. His dad's relatives were dead relatives, so it fell to Theo to sort through the junk of a man's whole life. The things his father used the night before his death — his comb, razor, belt — the next day became relics. In his father's bedroom, his shoes became occult. On his bed were the sheets where death arranged itself. Theo resented his dad's suit jacket for siting there on the chair back mimicking his shoulders. Jealous of his dad's bed for betraying that he still slept only on the left. Theo opened his dad's closet, his bathroom mirror, his bedside table, looking for the trinkets that sons collect from fathers they never see again.

He counted up his father's shirts and pants and laid them on the bed. He planned to give his clothes to the blind, his watch to the Salvation Army, his shoes to Sacred Heart. The blind made house calls, so in the end, most of his dad's shit went to the blind. Theo never managed to get rid of everything.

He found his father dead on a Monday night. Drunk and dead. Strangely, he was wearing just a hat. A grey fedora. Theo knew he was dead and not sleeping because when he slept he always cried. Theo was prepared. He went downstairs. Called the number on the fridge. When he came back into the room, he checked instinctively to see that his father was still dead. He shielded his eyes. In these last years he saw his dad naked many times. Even wiped his dad's ass. Suddenly he was shy of his father's nudity. As though through his death, his dad withdrew permission to be seen. Nudity is only shameful if you are not allowed to see it, Theo thought. He never walked in on his father with a woman, like his friends with moms had. There were never any women in the house.

Theo didn't want his father to be found naked like that. He went to the closet. Took out a pair of underwear. Pair of socks. Selected a beige shirt. Pair of navy pants. He dressed the dead man. He took off his hat. There was something inside the crown. He put the hat down on the pillow. He wanted the hospice men to find his father's dead, drunk body with the missing finger and severed genitals in a state of dignity. Theo knew full well that after they hauled him away, they would strip him naked on a metal slab and hose him down. Make a dick joke. Probably call in the janitor to have a peek. Then they would dress him up in his dead man's suit which Theo picked out a few days earlier sensing the end of the man, and laid on the chair by the closet. He felt guilty that he didn't have time to dry clean it as he had intended. His dad wouldn't have been buried with a stain on his breast pocket if his father had the foresight to die just a few days later. He didn't know if it was stupid to give a pair of underwear to the hospice people. Do they bury you without underwear?

Before the wake, the funeral director asked Theo if it was him who had made the alterations to the suit. What alterations? He told Theo that the pants had been rolled into cuffs and stitched crooked with red thread and the sleeves of the jacket had been turned inside.

TWELVE

Crowds amassed outside. The roofs were full. The crook superintendent of the housing project across the street was charging people to get up. Couple of bucks for front-row seats to the end of the world circus. People were taking shots of Deniz. Some were drinking. Pitching beer bottles across the street. Trying to provoke the leopard. Two guys were fighting. Get your fucking hand off my wife's ass. A graffiti artist had transformed the head of the huge cock spray-painted on Theo's house into a bishop from a chess set. There was an old man walking silently through the crowd with a sign written in black magic marker. Revelation 13:2. Theo went looked up the passage. The title of the passage was The Beast out of the Sea. And the beast which I saw was like a leopard, and his feet were like those of a bear, and his mouth like the mouth of a lion. And the dragon gave him his power and his throne and great authority. I saw one of his heads as if it had been slain, and his fatal wound was healed. And the whole earth was amazed and followed after the beast. Was this the end of the world Theo was waiting for? Another lunatic had a sign with Daniel 7:6. After this I kept looking, and behold, another one, like a leopard, which had on its back four wings of a bird; the beast also had four heads, and dominion was given to it. Theo thought it was possible that he himself was possessed by the devil.

THIRTEEN

TV news was going door to door interviewing neighbours. Showing the picture with the black eye. Digging up secrets about him. When he saw that, he actually considered, for the first time in many years, coming out. They didn't know he was a shut-in. He could have just been trapped in there. The water barring his exits. Or, he thought, throw yourself down the stairs. Break a leg. Be carried out as hero of the flood, the owner of the house which Deniz had chosen. He could do TV interviews on morning shows. Put his hand in the lap of female hosts during commercial breaks. Let Catalina see how well he was doing. How handsome he was. He was still young. But it was too late. The neighbours were talking. The world learned that his name was Theo. That his family name was Galli and that it was his father's house. They learned his father was a dead father. That he was some kind of musician. No. No one famous. His name was Adam. Not one of them had seen the woman of the house. What right did the world have to his secrets? They were telling it all wrong.

Theo thought of the secrets he and Catalina shared. Like when she told him she felt physical pain in her ovaries at emotional moments. Like weddings or concerts or sad movies. Even at a baptism once. He knew that Catalina's mom only bought her white bras and underwear as a way to guard against lost virginity. If her mother found colourful underwear in her drawer it was a sure sign that she was having sex with men. In the end, Theo's gift of black lingerie was never worn.

Not so much out of fear of her mother, but because she said black reminded her of the dead. Theo thought of his boyhood secrets. The sour green apple candies stolen from the gas station store in the fifth grade. Smoking the cigarettes of the moms of his friends. Skipping school after planning it since Nick's birthday. The birthday with the coins baked right into the cake when he almost choked to death on a quarter. Of course the funerals. Theo had funerals for things. Like his toy soldiers when a limb fell off. Other things too. The old mattress that he helped his dad drag to the street. It was the same Christmastime that they found the dead man in front of the mechanic shop on the corner just lying there by the side of the road and his father telling him that no, he's not dead he's just drunk, but he was dead.

Since Catalina left, there had been an amassing of new secrets. That his father would shit himself awake. That there are life-changing things discovered inside the hats of dead men. That he never ate the meat that Catalina froze with the days of the week written on little pieces of paper like an old lady leaving her husband at home to go off to die of ovarian cancer. That he was the only one there for his father's amputation. That he became a shut-in for seven years. That he failed three times at taking his own life.

FOURTEEN

On the day she disappeared, when Theo came home to an empty house, he had a premonition that she was gone for good. It was the smell of freshly cut hair in the upstairs bathroom. It wasn't until 3AM, after several frantic and unanswered calls that he had the balls to open her underwear drawer.

He missed the smell of Catalina. The orange blossom scent that lingered after she left the house. He missed the way Catalina was never heard before entering a room. Simultaneously appearing in the kitchen and in the bedroom. On that sad day, he felt it was so stupid being hungry. Warming up some soup. You're going to kill me, Catalina. I'm going to die. But Theo doesn't die. You can't ever kill a lonely man.

There were strange triggers. St. Eulalia subway station at night. Full moons. The names of tropical storms. Depending on the memory, he felt it in different places on his body. Her voice in his gut. Sex he felt in his ribs. His own body had phantom pains where she used to belong. Theo was so consumed by missing her that he became afraid of the lulls in his own sadness. Afraid that her body was forgetting his. Then he'd languish amongst the things she left behind, like the black lingerie in her underwear drawer, in order to trigger the pain.

One unexpected pain was that everywhere he went after their separation he had to answer for her disappearance. Three days after she left him, some old lady stopped him in the café to give him back the book she forgot. *Odi et Amo* by Catullus.

At the corner store the Korean sold him her Rothmans. The neighbour's kid asked where's her red bicycle. In the second-hand store she liked, they would talk with Theo to finish conversations with Catalina about the strange weather we're having and what does a dog mean in coffee grounds. Who was this lady? In her absence he learned the vastness of Catalina. Theo was secretly terrified of the day he'd be stopped by a stranger asking after children he never heard of.

Catalina's friend Sibyl or her sister Hilaria came over a couple times after it happened. Made him feel like he was bereaved. But in the end, they were just there to get Catalina's effects. Like she was a dead woman. Less shit for the shrine. Here is the scarf she left. Her iris earrings. Her child-size guitar.

FIFTEEN

Theo and Cat met because of the red swollen genitals of the female ovulating baboon. When Theo was going to class in university, a sign was posted on the door of the architecture building. Men Wanted. Sex Study. Cash. Meet Friday at 3 at The Prey.

The Prey was the nickname of the overcrowded old Neo-Gothic chapel which had been hollowed out and made into a student dining hall. Theo had to cut Early Bronze Age Near-Eastern Architecture to make the first meeting. The sex study participants could meet in the nave in the hour between lunch and dinner service.

A girl at the door took the first twelve men who signed up. Someone asked where's the girls. The women are already here. Chosen for their secondary sex characteristics, Theo supposed. They're waiting in the kitchen. Keep your pants on. They'll be coming out one by one. The women were numbered to avoid the inevitable sexual power of a woman's name. Avoiding the off-chance of an ex-lover or dead grandma. The men were told to each choose a cafeteria table. The men were also told that the women didn't know they were about to be judged on sexual attractiveness.

The rules. You must sit close to the woman, but not touch. Smelling distance. Strict pheromonal adoration. Forbidden topics of conversation. Politics. Sex. And keep your god to yourself. Three minutes a man. Then the women will rotate. Clockwise. You are encouraged to watch her walk. Look her up and down. Smell her hair. The women have been instructed not to take offence. You will not be told the categories of sexual attractiveness or the ranking system until after the three-minute conversations are all over and the women are back in the safety of the galley kitchen. It was only afterwards that Theo and the other men learned that the study was meant to see if men find women more sexually attractive when they are ovulating. But on that first day, Theo wondered how to count up a woman. Rank the sensory features of her face? Is there a sexual potency index? Wilcoxon–Mann Test? Measuring the degree of sexual arousal by the angle of erection?

Theo was nervous. He knew he'd fall in love with all of them. Theo expected them to be stripped of their street clothes, wearing white. Like a lunatic asylum. The women came out of hiding. It reminded Theo of a prison visitation. A girl sat beside him. She smelled like orange blossoms. Number One.

Sixteen

Women smell different when we want sex. Men can smell it. Like dogs smell fear. Fertile women are hornier. Swear to God it's a scientific fact. We are sexier when we can make babies. Makes perfect sense, no? There are no other sex studies like it, Number One told Theo over dinner at The Prey when the study was completed. The other studies are just men ogling photos of ovulating women. It doesn't work. The man and woman need to be face to face. The man needs to smell the woman. There needs to be a threat of vaginal penetration. The possibility of impregnation. This was Catalina. The organizer of the study. She volunteered because one of her friends got pregnant and dropped out at the last minute.

We gave the women hormone assays, Catalina said. We took a little vial of blood to predict ovulation. I had it done too, but I wasn't allowed to see the results till after. The idea for this study came out of her paper, Theatrics of Ovulation: Menstruation and the Birth of Love. Right then she was working on Vaginal Conspiracies: Pre-Literate Bleeding Strategies in Modern Ovulating Women. The test isn't about the man, Theo. Men are distractions. The test is about the woman. Simple question. Do women decorate themselves during estrus? Hair. Makeup. Shorter skirts. Heels. Lipstick. Earrings. Mascara. Boob job. Have you ever considered the female tendency to decorate the places where the body opens? Women decorate their vaginas too, Theo. Manicure pubic hair. Pierce the clit. Catalina called her vagina a liminal space. The body's boundary. Theo had never met anyone like her.

Can you smell the perfume I'm wearing? It's OK. Smell me, Theo. Perfume is the symbolic elaboration of pheromones. Perfume is meant to make you smell me. Not to smell the scent of the perfume, but my deeper scent. The animal smell.

Catalina picked up the flowers from the table. Theo brought her red roses. Why do men give flowers to women, Theo? Because flowers are genitals. The meeting place of sperm and egg. She smelled the flowers. Roses have both male and female reproductive organs. Most flowers are hermaphrodites. Years later he would hear this same sentence from his own dying father.

Theo, do you want to understand women? Then you have to understand the female olive baboon. When she's ovulating, her genitals swell up and turn red. The male baboons go sex crazy. The female has sex over and over. All different males. Of course she gets pregnant. But who's the father? This leads to father baboons killing newborns. The male has no connection to the offspring. The baby is not a daughter or son. It's just another mouth.

Human females at one stage of evolution might also have had some theatrical ovulation of their own. Maybe a blue vagina. Spotted breasts. But over time, ovulation hid itself inside the woman. Hidden even from herself. For men, that meant no more looking for colourful genitals. No more roving one woman to the next. Now the man's got to mate again and again with the same woman. He's got to wait on the egg. Pair-bonding, Cat called it. That's the Paleolithic way of saying fall in love. Now when a little baby boy is born, the man knows he's the father. At least he thinks he is. So he doesn't kill the boy. He loves his boy. Loves the mom. There you go. Birth of the family. There was just one problem with human culture. Menstrual blood.

These men had no concept of the sperm and the egg. The men thought they knew all the important things that came out of a woman. It came down to two female liquids. Blood or milk. If she's lactating, she can't get pregnant. If there's no blood, she might be pregnant. And if she is pregnant, she can't get pregnant. Only on their honeymoon would Theo learn that Catalina was an Irish twin. Her mother Berenice Chasta got pregnant with Cat right after her older sister Hilaria was born. Hilaria was born in March and Cat was born in December. But if a woman is bleeding, Cat continued, it's only a matter of time before she can get pregnant. So naturally, the bleeding woman attracts the men. All the men go off trailing blood. Just like the red genitals of the olive baboon.

One woman living in this pre-literate society recognized this. Maybe she lost her man to a bleeding female. And this woman, whoever she was, did the first symbolic cultural act in human history. She went out looking. Not for food or weapons or water. She went out looking for a colour. She went looking for red. Maybe berries. Maybe some red earth. She took that red colour and decorated herself. Between her legs. It was an artistic act. Like body art. Her man returned to her. Other men came. Soon other women realized that they all needed to paint their vaginas red. So they all did it.

Think about it. Why the theatrics? What do women need men for, Theo? Sex? A father figure for their children? No. They need men for meat. The men were the hunters. If the women had equal access to men, they would all be provided with meat. It was at this precise time in human evolution, the very same time as women learned to fake their periods, that men learned to kill big animals. They could hunt large cats in groups and not be killed. The men learned to outwit the animals. The women learned to outwit the men. Women had colluded to appear uniformly fertile. This was how women took control of men. A simple exchange. Sex for meat.

Remember, Theo, at this stage of human development, language did not yet exist. There were no arguments. Sex and food was the only human language. That was the only argument. The women learned that they could unanimously forbid sex at the same time until they were provided for. Theo asked how the women could all agree on a time to fake their period if they had no language. Easy. They let nature decide for them. They looked at the moon, Theo. They chose a time when they knew the men could hunt. Under a full moon, the men had the light to kill their prey. Menstruation, at that time of human evolution, was rare. Never monthly.

The women, in order to keep up this menstrual pageant, had to hide from the men. They needed to paint their vaginas red in private. So the men learned that bleeding women were to be left alone. Not to be touched. No sex. The blood was dangerous. Taboo. So, the men went off to hunt. The men outsmarted the big cats and killed them. Why didn't they devour their kill right then and there, Theo asked. That's such a male question, she said. They didn't eat the meat because they had been conditioned by the fake vaginal blood to know that blood was not to be touched. Never consumed. They had to return to the group. Clean the beast. What better way to remove the sight of blood from a dead animal than fire. It is no coincidence that this was the moment in human history when our species learned to cook. So, fake vaginal blood led to the birth of cooking. Theo looked down at his food and Cat laughed loud.

Do you want me to keep going, Theo? Yes, I do. At first the fake blood was a survival trick. Men were swindled. Out of sex and meat. But all it would take was one man to see one woman painting herself red to ruin the whole damn thing. And one man must have seen. Maybe by accident. Maybe through his own cunning. Then another. Until all of them knew. But the fake blood didn't die out. What was once a trick became collusion. The painted blood was important for the hunt. Whenever the women decorated their vaginas with fake blood, the men killed their prey. Blood calls to blood. The fake blood of fertility blessed the hunt. The man and woman still couldn't speak to each other with words. But they could love, Catalina said.

Think of the holes of human bodies, Theo. They are also the sensory organs or erogenous zones. Survival isn't everything. What about desire? Evolution doesn't make the perfect human. Some men like small tits. Small hips. Shaved vagina. Pre-fertile traits. And even today when the male gets the female, what does he do? He covers his penis in rubber. How's that for the procreative instinct? And that barely matters anyway, because she's already taking a little pill every day that stops ovulation. Most of the women you see walking down the street have no eggs.

If you're on the pill, you don't have a period. There's no building up then breaking down of the endometrium. Should be no vaginal bleeding. But what do we do instead? We fake it. In the pack there are three weeks of anti-egg pills. But did you know, Theo, that there is one week of sugar pills? What are the sugar pills there for? They put them in the box so that women can fake their period. Maybe she doesn't want the male to know. Fifty-thousand years later and nothing's changed. That blood is fake. It's withdrawal bleeding. Fake fertility. But come on Theo, the male knows the female is infertile. He knows she's on it. Nowadays he doesn't care. It's her infertility, not her fertility, which draws him to her. He doesn't want the threat of children. We are exhibiting behaviour of a dying species, Theo.

SEVENTEEN

There was a question Theo was dying to ask Catalina on their first date. Did I predict your ovulation? Her answer was simple. Why else do you think I agreed to go out with you? Theo was a natural at picking ovulating women, it turned out. Catalina's mother Berenice, who crossed over on foot with her two daughters and understood pain, thought the whole business with the blood was crazy. It only reminded her of the Hemorrhaging Woman, one of the many sacred nameless in the Holy Bible. The Hemorrhaging Woman was cured of 12 years of vaginal bleeding by touching the cloak of Christ. Three miscarriages, Catalina, and I never complained. I picked out girls' names for them all. Sabina, Bellona, and Aelia. The only other advice Berenice could give her daughter was don't plant roses when you are menstruating, they won't grow.

EIGHTEEN

Theo proposed to Cat one year later on the roof of The Prey. Cat kept the key to the back door. They snuck up after hours. Catalina picked out the ring herself from a vintage shop. She insisted on actinolite. Incredible for its metaphysical capacity, the jeweller told them. He explained the chatoyancy phenomenon. The cat's eye effect. Catalina picked one with a sterling silver band. Theo came back for the ring the next day. It came with a little blue booklet of the gemological properties of cat's eye. Among the criteria were Hardness (5.5 to 6 on the Mohs scale) and Cleavage (Good).

Cat kissed Theo with an open mouth. She always kissed like that. Theo thought of their first kiss. Up there on that very roof. With Cat it was never just a kiss. You were participating in the history of the symbolism of mouths. Kissing has its origins in pre-mastication. Kiss feeding, she called it. In the animal world there are all sorts of courtship feeding. Like the sperm gifts of certain butterflies or the sex gifts of spiders. She put on the ring and pulled him down over her on the roof. Bite my lip, Theo. As hard as you can. Theo drew blood.

They went to see Fr. Baldacchino at Sacred Heart. They were separated into different rooms so the priest could make sure Catalina wasn't pregnant and it wasn't shotgun and that they weren't related by blood. They signed up for marriage classes where an 80-year-old volunteer widow taught them how to avoid conception the natural way by testing for cervical mucus with the thumb and index finger. At ovulation, the consistency of the vaginal mucus is like egg whites, the old lady said.

They got married in the lower chapel in the basement of Sacred Heart. Cat never did find a dress in sulphate red made of cactus cloth and embroidered with sunflowers. In the end she went white with a red flower in her hair. They left the church as man and wife. The families were waiting on the steps to Sacred Heart. He passed through the door where Cat's sister Hilaria was standing. Theo felt something smash over his head. He looked over at Cat to see her mother raise an egg into the air and bring it down over her daughter's head. Birdseed covered her hair and scattered on the ground. Cat burst out laughing. The little kids at the wedding took the rest of the eggs from a basket that Hilaria was carrying and chased each other up and down the steps of the church. Cat brushed the birdseed off his hair. These are *cascarones*, Theo. Something we do after the weddings in my town. The yolks were emptied through a small hole in the top and filled up with seed. The tiny hole in the top was covered with red tissue paper.

After the wedding they went on a honeymoon. A week in Mexico. She insisted he visit the place she was born. The place where many years later the hurricane would begin as a mouthful of wind. Theo and Cat walked the street hand in hand. Stopping to breathe into each other's mouths. They walked to the mouth of an abandoned silver mine with the sign San Ramón. Cat used to play down there as a girl. All children's games here have the threat of death. Now there was a boy selling tickets for a tour of the mine. The boy was no older than nine. He took them down talking facts that he practiced at home with his mom. Cat translated *vientre de la tierra*. Belly of the earth. Cat and Theo followed the little boy down stone steps. He took Cat's hand to touch certain parts of the wall. Then the stairs stopped. There was a rope running along the wall and they held on to go deeper. They reached the bottom. 60 metres down. When they came out of the mouth of the mine, there was a little table lined with souvenirs. Cat bought a little figure of San Ramón with a padlock on his lips. She handed the money to the boy. *Preguntas?* Yes, Theo had a question. Why is the mine called San Ramón? The mine is named after a real man. Ramón Nonato. The legend is that his mother died when he was still in her belly. And she was buried with the baby inside her. His father couldn't sleep that night. So he went to the cemetery to cry for her. But he heard crying that was not his own. He dug up his wife's body. The crying was coming from inside her. He cut open her belly and pulled out his son: Ramón. He is the patron of miners. Cat asked what about your father. Is he a miner? *Yo no tengo padre.*

After Theo and Cat made love, she read aloud the poetry of Catullus, the Roman poet loved by the ancient orgiastic cults. Then rising, the ground wet with blood, he was transformed, a woman with her delicate white hands sounding the tympanum, the tympanum singing praise through sacred trumpets raised to goddess Cybele, mysterious mother of a sexless race.

As is always the case with the most beautiful women, Catalina's mother was against the wedding. Catalina was born with no father. Just as Theo believed he was born with no mother. When Catalina was old enough to know she had been abandoned forever, she asked for her father. She remembered the conversation well. *Escúchame bien, mija.* You have one last name. Chasta. You have no father, her mother swore. You hatched. Like an egg.

NINETEEN

When they got home from the honeymoon, the university cut off Catalina's grant money for research into primal vaginal blood. They claimed the results were faked. Somehow they uncovered that Catalina participated as a volunteer in her own study and hired her girlfriends to be paid participants. Evidently one of the women talked. Breaking the female collusion. Her thesis was dismissed by the older professors as the hysteria of a woman.

Catalina was onto something new. The genital conspiracies of expectant mothers in pair-bonded heterosexual relationships. Married pregnant women bored of their husband's genitals. Unable to get the backing of the university after three attempts, she brought the study into their new home. It was a small three-storey. Theo's father said the roof would do. Friday evenings at eight, four pregnant women showed up with their haploid males. Sybil, Catalina's friend from the sex study, survived from the original group. She was impregnated by Alexander, a boy she met during the study. Cat and Sybil stayed friends. Theo liked to be out of the house during the vaginal conspiracies.

Like in all sexual studies, the men and women were separated into different rooms. The participants filled out invasive forms about sexual frequency and duration. Theo thought Cat had ripped off some questions from the Catholic marriage questionnaire. Then she added her own. Turn-ons. Turn-offs. Put an x in the box. Then the questions for the men.

Have you watched your partner while urinating? Have you urinated on your partner during a sexual interaction? Do you desire to be urinated upon? Spat on? Can you recognize the smell of your sexual mate? Have you blindfolded your sexual mate? If blindfolded, and without the use of your hands, are you able to distinguish the taste of different parts of her body?

TWENTY

The end of the marriage of Theo and Catalina began on the afternoon of the egg. Sybil brought over the newborn. A three-day-old girl they called Cleo after first calling her Samantha Beth, then Phoebe. Cat's sister Hilaria and a few other women friends were there in the aftermath of the birth. Sybil was an open woman. She insisted that Catalina was present for the delivery. Theo mocked this. He was reminded that you know nothing of women's pain. The real reason that the women were all congregating in Theo's dining room was for the placenta party. Catalina's idea. She was now a placentophagist. Not so much because of nutrition, but because of the placenta's value as a female conspiratorial organ. Catalina claimed the placenta holds special power because it's a blood boundary. Stopping the mother's blood mixing with the baby's. The fate of the baby mimics the fate of the afterbirth. That and eating it helps your tits not to sag when you stop breastfeeding.

Theo came home right in the middle of it. Catalina made eutherian organ smoothies. Theo said hi. Cleo was asleep in her bassinet upstairs in the spare room. The room they planned as a nursery. Theo painted it red because he thought red was a male and female colour. He was enthusiastically invited to look at the baby. But no one followed as he made his way up the stairs. Theo went in to look at the sleeping baby girl. She was beautiful. Everything on her was pink. Theo thought about the gender of colours. He went back downstairs and listened in on talk of breastmilk. A placenta cookbook.

Twisted ovaries. He learned that vaginas of redheads are more likely to tear in childbirth. After half an hour, at the request of the women, Theo went in to check on little Cleo the second time. That was when he saw it. A white bowl filled with water on the floor under the bassinet. Inside the bowl were two eggs. Theo knelt down to check that the eggs were eggs. This was strange.

He woke two times that night. Theo was thinking about the eggs. He didn't say shit about the eggs to Catalina. At 3AM he got out of bed and went to the spare room. The bowl with the eggs was gone. Theo thought what the hell. The next day, when Catalina was out, he walked into the other bedroom. Gave a quick little check under the bed. Nothing. Of course he couldn't help but check under their own bed for suspicious shelled fetuses. For some reason, he still couldn't bring himself to ask Catalina. There was something clandestine about the eggs. That night, after they had sex, Theo brought it up. Catalina laughed. Oh, that's just something they do back home. It's to protect babies or old people against *mal de ojo*. You know, the evil eye. No, Theo didn't know the evil eye. Not yet.

Catalina said that sometimes the egg would turn black. For adults, usually women, red veins appear. For children, sometimes the yolk bubbles. And did the egg do anything? Yes, actually it did a little. Did it bubble? No, it turned black a bit. So Cleo is OK then? For now yes. Catalina went to sleep. Theo did not. He thought, what can I know about you if I didn't know that you are the kind of woman who puts two eggs in a bowl of water under a baby? He figured it's the kind of thing you tell someone right away.

The egg changed Theo. He didn't quite know why. Him knowing seemed to change Catalina a little too. On the construction site, building the skeletons of bedrooms, he tried to figure out the egg. He heard enough of Catalina's anthropology to puzzle it out. An egg is laid by a female. A baby is laid by a female. The egg is like the baby then. So, if you can get the evil into the egg, then you can get the evil out of the baby. Simple demonic mathematics. In the end, it made perfect sense to him. He started thinking, what is the double of me? What could I use to suck out the evil? What would turn black under my bed?

TWENTY-ONE

A month after the eggs, Theo came into the bedroom. Catalina was already asleep. From the colour of the traffic light he made his way to the bed. Looked at his sleeping wife with her hands clasped tight in front of her mouth. Theo thought, your last waking feeling hardens on your face as you sleep. Like catalepsy. That's when he noticed the tiny droplets of blood. He had to wait until the light turned green in order to confirm it. Little drops of blood formed on the pillow around her hands. He turned on the bedside lamp. Shook Cat. Cat screamed when she saw them. Five tiny bugs crawling on the pillow. She went straight into the shower. Left Theo to crush the bedbugs. He unfolded the sheets to catch the bugs roaming his marriage bed. He found another one under the pillow. Six. Another two around the waist and genital area. Seven. Eight. And five by the feet. Thirteen. He stripped the bed and put the sheets in a black plastic garbage bag.

Catalina told Theo to throw her panties in the bag. She got new underwear from the drawer and went downstairs. Theo stripped to his ass and looked in the mirror. He examined his body. There was one on his left arm. In the bend of his elbow. Another bite on the top of his left foot. Five, he heard from downstairs. Five fucking bites. The bedbugs preferred Catalina. Sweet skin, his dad used to say when he came home with mosquito bites as a boy. Theo vacuumed the top of the mattress naked. Then he flipped the queen onto the floor. There, under the mattress, resting on the slat, was a small, square wooden carving of the Virgin Mary wearing a red mantle. He grabbed the Virgin. Catalina appeared naked in the doorway. What the hell is this, Cat? Don't talk like that. That's *la virgen*. What is la veer-hen doing under our bed? It's nothing bad. Who fucking cares, Theo? I have bedbug bites on my tits. Theo wouldn't let the virgin alone. If you put something red under the mattress, Catalina explained, it keeps the passion in the bedroom. So you're a fucking witch then. Fuck you, Theo. What are the bedbugs for, Cat?

Theo couldn't live in that house with human parasites in his bed and placentas in the blender. Never knowing when he'd wake to a red votive candle burning for a dead relative. His house was booby-trapped with bird embryos and household gods. After the fight — Catalina threw two eggs at him — he went to sleep at his dad's. His dad asked if everything was all right. Theo told him that they fumigated. And that Catalina was staying with her friend to help with the baby.

These were curses, Theo thought. How are you supposed to conceive with *la virgen* lying under your wife? A long time they'd been trying. Nothing.

Twenty-two

Cat wouldn't come home until they fumigated. The exterminator brought in a Great Dane. The dog's name's Benedict. Benedict sniffed Theo's testicles. Nothing in there boy, said the exterminator. My name's Don. Theo, right? Benedict will sniff out those cocksuckers dead or alive. He let the dog go and Benedict bounded upstairs. The exterminator followed the dog with a silver canister. Theo asked what's the dog for. Bedbugs are hard to get. Even if you kill all but two they'll breed like motherfuckers. It's real fucked up too how they do it. The boy bedbug stabs the girl bedbug right in her belly with his little prick. Then he shoots his sperm direct to her abdominal cavity. That's what they call traumatic insemination. Bugs are fucked. Half the time the girl bug is so starved that she'd rather cannibalize the boy than fuck him. The dog started barking at the bed like crazy. The exterminator gave it to the bugs with the canister. That's why some of the males fake dead, you know. Take the nursery web. That's a spider. He plays dead. Then just when the female gets up close he jumps up. Fucks her. He's got to do it. Man's got no choice. You want to hear something real fucked up? He flipped the mattress over. Benedict was going wild. So let's imagine one male bug, he's fucking the female, OK. All of sudden he jerks to one side and rips his little prick right off. Plugging the bug's pussy so she can't mate with another male. It almost guarantees pregnancy. The exterminator finished up. Theo paid cash. Find any more of these cocksuckers and give Don a call. That

way I can tell you about the virgin birth of pit vipers or about
this all female species of lizard. Fuck, there's a lot of fatherless
lizards out there.

TWENTY-THREE

Cat came home that night. Theo told her that he wanted to have a baby. Right now? Yes, right now. He made love to her in the downstairs tub. They had sex in every room in the home over the next few months. Except the bedroom. Theo felt an incredible potency. Fucked until his two balls sagged. Nothing happened. They did everything to check for pregnancy. Those drugstore piss tests. Even observing the behaviour of Theo's dad's cat to see if he reacted differently with Catalina. Eventually, Catalina dragged him to a doctor. Doctor said don't worry, get an ovulation kit and see. Theo got the kit at a 24-hour drugstore near their house. He also bought a bottle of mineral water and shaving cream because he felt strange. And a little notepad. Inside the kit were twenty tests all individually wrapped. Cat peed on one. They counted three minutes and didn't talk. Theo went to check. In the little window was an O. O means nothing. She had to keep trying until she pissed a happy face. They tried the next day and the day after. Keeping their hopes up for the surge of luteinizing hormone. A couple weeks later and that little smiley face appeared. They fucked like crazy over the next 48 hours. Nothing.

Three months of O and smiles and nothing and the doctor ordered tests. Theo had to jerk off in a little plastic cup with his name and birthday on it. The doctor told him that for the test, your penis cannot come in contact with Catalina's vagina. It has to be a pure sample. He made Cat get out of the house. He laughed because it took him a really long time. He kept focusing on that plastic cup with his name and birthday. How was he supposed to get it in there? Then it happened. He got it in there all right. Wiped up. Zipped up. He was fully dressed. Even had his shoes on. The doctor told him you only have 45 minutes to get the ejaculate to the lab before the sample degrades. He put the cup into the biohazard sandwich bag the doctor gave him. He had a brown lunch bag ready and waiting so no one could see what he was carrying. Theo ran out of the house. He felt strange carrying a bag of his sperm down the street. Passing all the places he knew. One of his old friends noticed him in the street. Theo let the cock crow. A homeless man asked him for some change. He got on the subway at St. Eulalia Station. Carrying the bag in his lap. Holding it with two hands. He felt like he robbed a bank. There in that cup of spunk, he carried the whole history of his family. His entire lineage trapped in a plastic cup in a brown lunch bag riding the subway. There was a religious tract left on the seat next to his. He opened to Baby Jesus.

There were a few awkward nights between Catalina and Theo after that. He hadn't told her about the experience. That he read Born of a Virgin on the subway. That he was humiliated in the waiting room. Everyone and their little bags. That the secretary talked too loud. He only told Cat that he dropped his semen off. They continued to routinely have sex. They kept at the O and the smiley face. But both of them carried a new small shame. There was something wrong with one of their genitals. They had sex with the light off that night.

The results came back for Catalina first. She was fine. Better than fine even. In the doctor's words, you are a very fertile woman. *Entonces, son tus huevos*, Catalina tried to joke. Theo didn't get it. Theo was preparing for the worst. It was his balls that were the problem. He knew it. The results came in a couple days later. You have an extremely high sperm count, Theo. There are no fertility issues with either of you. They were ordered to keep having sex on schedule while the doctor made an appointment with a sexual reproduction specialist.

Catalina rode him with extra prowess. Like a fertility goddess. Moaning wildly. There was a certain self-awareness though. No reckless abandon like in the old days. None of the openness of their lovemaking on the roof when he proposed. The burden of fertility weighed on them. But the sign of their monthly failure of love was blood. After a particularly heavy period — Catalina blamed her darker blood on the gravitational pull of the moon — they stopped having sex. First for a few days. Then weeks on end. Cat was reading Federico García Lorca in bed. She translated for him. It's all right if a man doesn't look for his joy in tomorrow morning's jungle of blood. The sky has shores where life is avoided and there are bodies that shouldn't repeat themselves in the dawn. Cat was trying to console him with a poem about a homosexual.

Theo faked sick on the day of the specialist appointment and Catalina knew it. When three months went by without the two touching each other, Theo started thinking about it.

TWENTY-FOUR

Vas deferens. The pamphlet gave the literal translation of the Latin. Vessel to carry away. Dr. Magliochetti came in. He remembered Theo's father. Penile cancer, right? The doctor went through the routine medical hoodoo. Checking his eyes, ears, mouth. His senses then his heart. He checked the weight of Theo. The young nurse took blood and his urine cup. Then he sat down. In his explanation of the procedure, Dr. Magliochetti used the words severed and sealed. Stupid question, but will I become feminine? No, your testicles will still be making testosterone. Will I still come? You can still ejaculate, but there will be no sperm in it. So Doctor, if the surgery doesn't eliminate the sperm, where does it go? Does it just build up down there? Won't they blow? Don't worry, Theo. The body breaks it down. It gets absorbed into the bloodstream. Theo was terrified by the idea of seminal blood. He imagined that he could impregnate through bleeding like in some ancient Roman cult. Won't the sperm poison my blood? No, eventually the body learns to see the sperm as hostile. Like an intruder in the body. Then kills it off. Like a virus? Yes. Your sperm will be like a virus.

He talked to Catalina about it. Showed her the pamphlet. Just a twenty-minute procedure. A couple of incisions. Shaved testicles. Then we won't have to worry about it. A burden lifted. Catalina was furious at first. Cursed him in Spanish. *Deshuevado.* But alone she read the clinic pamphlet. Theo rode the subway far from his house. He got off at a random stop. He was looking to know nobody. Theo went into a used bookstore and found the section for health and medical books. He looked for surgery. There was only one book. *The History of Surgery.* He flipped though the book. Something caught his eye. Catgut suture. At one time the fibre of animal intestines was used to make strings for surgery and musical instruments like guitars and cellos and violins.

TWENTY-FIVE

Theo told Cat to pack. He didn't let her double-check the stove. They went to the end of the street and got on the all-night bus with the other drunks. One by one everyone stumbled off. This was their last chance. If this didn't work, Theo was going through with the surgery. Theo and Cat were alone at the back of the bus as it left the city for the airport. Theo bought two 6:50AM tickets to Cat's hometown where they spent their honeymoon.

On the flight Cat slept off the wine. The idea of the trip was spontaneous. Theo couldn't sleep in the air so when they took off he looked for his rooftop like a little boy. Outside the tiny airport she hailed a green and white cab. The air smelled like orange blossoms. Cat chatted with the cabbie. Theo heard the word *luna*. The word *hijos*. He listened for *deshuevado* or *virgen*. A dog ran behind the taxi as they pulled up to Hotel Aquarius. Theo tried to remember if the word he was thinking of was *estrella* or *extraña*. Cat went in and asked for room 930. He felt like a primitive man or baboon returning to mate in the same place. They ended up in 650 which was exactly the same. After the perfunctory sex in the hotel bed, Theo passed out.

Twenty-six

Theo opened his eyes in the hotel and saw the black constellation hanging in the air. He tried to rub out the black stars in his eyes. Cat was already dressed. She didn't tell him where they were going. He would never have agreed. They went into a tiny little office with green walls. In the corner were a pair of parakeets. He couldn't tell if they were boys or girls. The cage was lined with pages from soft-core porn magazines. A woman came out from the back and hugged Catalina. She brought them into a little room with a medical bed with stirrups and a mattress on the floor in the corner. There was a row of empty baby food jars on the windowsill with the labels peeled off. He'll be here in a minute.

A man came in and greeted Theo with a big moist hand and Cat with a kiss on the cheek. He looked back at Theo's blue eyes and switched to English. So, little Cat's come back. And you want to have a boy? Sit down. Don't worry. Children are easy.

I have a patient who has sex with at least 21 different men every week. She believes that female semen is venomous if not released in sex. I have another girl who never takes her medication. She insists on leaving lit cigarettes in front of her little statue of Santa Muerte to cure her vaginal infection and get her husband back. She told me just never let Santa Muerte see you naked. Another girl prays to the severed head of Saint Vitalis. The patron of genital disease.

Just today I had a girl who orgasms without pleasure. I have an ex-nun who masturbates at canonical hours. As you can see, the job of gynecologist is more confessor than doctor. I have a premenopausal woman who rushes to see me every time she has her periods, which she calls *mi santo*. The worst I ever saw was a stone baby. The mother was so poor. She miscarried. She didn't have money for a doctor. The fetus was not small enough for her body to expel or absorb. For 25 years it stayed inside her. The woman's body treated it like a foreign object. Over time, the fetus calcified. She was old when she came to see me. The pain was too much. I sent her for surgery. At 61 years old she gave birth to a stone baby. Theo thought of the coin he swallowed when he was a kid.

The reason that Cat dragged Theo to her girlhood gynecologist was because of his reputation that he could guarantee boys. The woman who greeted them came back into the room holding a hospital gown. Catalina changed behind the curtain. The doctor told Theo that the nurse was his wife. Twenty-five years, he said. The wife left the room and came back wheeling a cart of implements. Vaginal tools. Lie down, Catalina. She put her feet into the stirrups. Theo watched the doctor pull on plastic gloves. He picked something off the tray that looked like the mouth of a steel bird. The wife took up her position over the doctor's shoulder. Keeping an eye on those moist hands. Theo averted his eyes as the doctor bent between Cat's legs. He looked at the decorative bars on the windows. It was a floral pattern with the ends of the vines designed to penetrate human flesh. The doctor's head disappeared completely. When he came up he pulled off the gloves and helped Cat up. Theo wanted to go. Now please lie down on the mattress. On your stomach, please. The doctor knelt down and loosened the gown to expose Cat's back. The wife brought over two baby food jars and a lighter. The doctor picked up a cotton ball with a pair of tweezers and dipped it in rubbing alcohol. He lit the ball. Stuck it into the baby food jar. Pulled it out. Put the jar upside down on Cat's lower back. It stuck to her skin. One more jar. He looked at Theo. The jars are going to bring the blood to the surface. This will stimulate blood flow to the waist. Increasing the chance of conception.

The doctor removed the jars and Cat changed. The doctor and his wife went into the front room. Cat hugged Theo and they laughed under their breath. He wants to talk to us. They sat down at a little desk in the other room. There were no other patients. The doctor rested those hands open on top of the desk. The wife stood over his shoulder.

All right Catalina, listen carefully. Wash your vagina with two tablespoons of baking soda mixed with a litre of water. It diminishes your female acid. He looked at Theo. The more acid the greater the possibility of conceiving a girl. After your period count 10 days. No sex from day 10 to day 18. The feminine sperm are more resistant than the masculine sperm. So have sex continuously between day 4 and day 9. You will have a boy.

The wife walked them into the street. The sun was strong. She hugged Cat and slipped something into her hand. Cat tucked it into her purse.

Twenty-seven

Theo watched Cat for a long time. Thigh-high in the ocean. There were two small circles on her lower back. It was getting late and the waves were enormous. She waited until a wave came and dove in head long. Theo thought about the gravitational pull of the moon. He reached over to Catalina's towel and grabbed her purse. He searched with his hand. It was a little necklace. Child size. He held it up. Dangling in front of him was a small charm of a penis. Theo looked up for Cat and watched her disappear inside the wave. He kept his eyes on the very spot in the ocean that swallowed up his wife. He watched as she reappeared. Catalina turned to him. She hadn't looked back at him once. He couldn't hear her but he knew that she screamed. Cat kicked her way out of the water. Fell onto the sand. Theo dropped the charm and ran to her. She was holding the inside of her thigh. She screamed *agua mala*. The mothers that were still on the beach ran and yelled to the water. Little children came out of the ocean and crowded Cat. One mother hauled her little boy out of the water from under his arms, pushed her way through, and set him down beside Cat. The mother pulled her son's trunks down and held onto the boy's penis. At first the boy refused. Cat told Theo move. The two women had an understanding. Cat opened her legs a little and the boy urinated on her thigh. Theo heard the word *doloroso* and the word *truco*. Not until the crowd dispersed did Cat look at Theo. It's a jellyfish sting. Theo didn't know what to do. He never saw her bit before. He got her to her feet and they walked back to their towels. He tucked the phallic charm back into her purse. Cat sent Theo in for some ice.

When he came back out, the woman was sitting next to Cat. The lady didn't look up at him. Theo made out *embarazada*. He thought the word meant embarrassed the first time he heard it. He watched the penis boy build a sandcastle and kick it over. A few kingdoms later, the boy came up to Theo with his red pail and shovel and said something. Theo looked to Cat for a translation. He wants to know if you want him to bury you.

TWENTY-EIGHT

That night in bed, Theo examined the bite. There were thin lines across her thigh. They looked like they were formed beneath her skin. Like the inside of her body was clawed. What did that lady say to you? Cat laughed. Tell me. She wanted to know if I was pregnant. Why? She said that sea creatures are attracted by pregnancy. She said that if I want to be safe, I should swim in the river instead, where the water creatures are repulsed by pregnancy.

Cat turned onto her back and lifted her book above her head. She always read in bed like that. She brought *Oedipus Rex* to the beach. Cat loved the Sphynx. Head and breasts of a woman. Body of a lioness. Devouring men. Cat got into Greek drama after she used *Lysistrata* in one of her university papers. The play where all the women refuse sex until their husbands end the war. She closed her book and looked at Theo. Pregnancy is like an ancient Greek tragedy. Think about it, Theo. Pregnancy has three acts too. The play starts with the protasis. Then the catastasis. The third trimester of the play ends with the catastrophe.

She sat up in bed. Do you want to try a riddle, Theo? Cat sat on her knees. If you get it wrong, I'll eat you alive. The answer is man, Cat. No, no. This is another riddle. There's another version of the story. There's a second riddle. Ready? There are two women. The first woman gives birth to the other woman. That newborn woman then gives birth to her own mother. Who are they?

I don't know Cat. That's the wrong answer, Theo. She pounced on him. Biting his neck and his shoulders. He played at fighting off the Sphynx. Cat cocked her head to one side and bit down hard into his chest. Then she pulled off his underwear and straddled him backwards. There were two small circles looking back at him from her skin. As they made love, Theo could tell from behind that she was silently crying.

When Cat was asleep he went into the washroom and looked at the red oval on his chest. That night, Theo dreamed of ejaculating onto an egg which turned into a disembodied eye. In his dream he bent over and it turned to stone. The next morning the bruise on his chest turned black.

TWENTY-NINE

Theo and Cat took the red-eye home. Theo took the window seat again. He ordered a child-size bourbon and looked outside. Cat didn't drink. He looked out at the night. Theo thought because he was in the air he could find the constellation Cancer. He tried to place it somewhere between the lion and the twins.

Cat put her head in Theo's lap. She was mouthing the words to a Spanish song. Theo heard *abandona* and *cielito lindo*. What's that mean, Cat? A bird that abandons her first nest, Little Pretty Sky, then finds it lived in by another, deserves her loss.

Cat woke only when they touched the ground. She slept on Theo the whole way. At the airport Theo answered all the questions about their identities and their home and the reason for their trip. The taxi played Coltrane's *Interstellar Space* album. They got from Mars to Leo and Jupiter Variation was just about to start when they pulled up at the house. Theo gave the driver a big tip. He dragged the suitcase up the stairs and put it onto the bed. He hadn't slept and his eyes were two dark circles.

Cat unzipped the suitcase and threw it open. There, from among the pairs of underwear, came a small red crab. Almost dead. It scuttled out of the suitcase, onto the bed, and disappeared under the sheets.

THIRTY

On the operating table, Theo asked if this how they did animals. The doctor told him relax. It will all be over before you know it. And it was. Twenty minutes and it was over. An entire history all tied up. Severed and sealed. It was an out-patient procedure. He got dressed. The doctor told him seven days before sex. I know that sounds like a lifetime. Any questions? Theo asked, does it hurt to get an erection? Can the incision open? Can my balls fall off? Nothing like that, the doctor told him. You'll be sore down there for a while, but the real reason you need to wait is because of the possibility of pregnancy. There is still sperm that has to make its way out of your body. It sometimes takes up to twenty ejaculations. Make sure your partner is taking birth control. Don't worry. You have an appointment in seven days, and we will check to see if all the sperm is gone.

Not being able to have sex that night, Theo satiated himself by sucking her breasts. His balls hurt. He wanted to put a cold egg right on his testicles. He fell asleep with the taste of her breasts in his mouth. Next morning, Theo thought his own breath smelled different, the way your mouth sours during a sick spell. Cat treated him like a sick boy. She took extra care not to wake him. He watched as she put on her clothes in the dark, then tiptoed out of the room. Walking on eggshells. When he woke up, she brought him soup. That night she read Catullus to him before bed. Catalina dreamed almost every day that week.

Theo read over the sheet of side effects. Blood in semen. Bleeding in scrotum. Granuloma from leaking sperm. Pregnancy. He wondered if women experience symptoms of vasectomy in their partner the way some men experience pregnancy with cramps and cravings and bloating of the belly. Are a woman's dreams a side effect of vasectomy? I dreamed about your mother last night and she was dead, Cat told him. Theo only cared if he was in the dream. Looking for any trace of himself inside her. He thought of when they first fell in love, and how he sometimes lied about dreaming of her. In those days she'd ask for every detail of the dream like a shaman priestess. Decoding water imagery. Extolling the significance of colours or animals.

Theo rested for the first day after surgery, but they went out for dinner every other night that week. One night they went to a Turkish café. Cat read the coffee grounds. In Theo's cup, Cat saw a house. That's a symbol of the soul. Cat got a bird in her cup. Animal shapes are important because they tell you human characteristics. Cat called him pet names. It was like they were re-enacting their first days together. Catalina even offered Theo some cake from her own spoon like she used to. They walked down the street. Passed strip clubs and upstairs massage parlours. Cat pointed out a sex shop. They never went to a sex shop before. Inside they split up. Theo wandered down an aisle of cocks. Cat called him over laughing. Look. Cat Whip. The box said Cat O'Nine Tails.

THIRTY-ONE

In seven days, they gave Theo another plastic cup. There was a small room with plain walls. Theo shut the door. The lock was gummed. Just Theo and his cock. There were magazines. An issue of *Men Only*. *Men's World*. One in French called *Lui*. There was a really old one called *Modern Man*. Theo thought of all the guys squeezing out their very last drops to these glossy vaginas. He stopped at the image of a girl with a golden tan. On all fours. The result of the test confirmed it. Theo had reached a state of azoospermia. Nine months later, the marriage was dead.

Day Three

ONE

Marry me Theo. Marry me Theo. Theo woke up to chanting. He opened his eyes and saw the constellation of black stars hovering below the ceiling. He peered outside. Some girls had marry me signs. Theo got a hard-on. He looked out at the crowd. Then he noticed the masks.

Somebody had gotten the idea to make copies of the only picture they had of him. People were wearing Theo masks. Theo with a black eye. The guy selling the masks was also selling stuffed leopards. Might have been cheetahs. Theo wondered how much the masks were going for. On TV, there were still images of Theo and Deniz. The screen split half man, half animal. The news started calling him Leopard Man. The crowd was enormous and unwieldy now. The graffiti artist re-imagined the cock on the front of the house once again. It was turned into the mast of a sinking ship. Religious people were out there with signs too. Going end of the world crazy. Blaming the flood on blood moons, genital diseases, the alignment of the stars, gas prices, the faggots. Theo was worried that they were going to storm the house and kill Deniz like a sacred animal. Parade him through the streets then devour him.

Theo realized he was starving. Deniz was going to starve him out. He couldn't say how much longer he could hold out. It occurred to Theo that the animal was also starving to death on his roof.

To stave off the hunger he chose the largest wall in his dad's bedroom. He dragged away the dresser. Took down the large mirror that was hanging there. He went to the garage to check for paint. He came back up with a bucket of roof tar and a brush. There was a warning label on the side. Do not use if pregnant. Fumes harmful to human fetal cells. He sat down and put the bucket between his legs and pried off the lid. It stank of rotten egg. Theo angled the TV so that he had a good shot of Deniz. Then he dipped in the brush. Theo started with the head. He painted the outline in that burning black tar. Life size. He moved on to the long body. The legs. The claws. Theo worked frantically. Dipping the brush and stabbing tar roses all over the body. Theo went back to the head. He painted in the black nose that looked like a female pubic triangle and that black line down to the mouth that looked like the space between a woman's thighs. Theo saw female genitalia in the shape of the leopard's facial features. Seemed like something his dad would say. He remembered that the female reproductive tract looks like a ram's head with fallopian tube horns. Then he dipped the brush again and painted two large human eyes. Theo climbed up on the bed to get a look at him. He jumped back down. Something was missing. With one long continuous stroke, Theo added two balls and an enormous animal cock.

Two

A truck was winding its way through the wreckage of St. Eulalia Street. Moving down the road in fits and starts. Laying on the horn to disperse the crowds. Theo looked out from the corner of the attic bedroom window. On the flatbed was a large cage. Theo caught a flash of gold skin. He knew that it was female. Men got out. Surrounded the cage. They carried guns. Yes, she was female. Theo listened for any subtle changes in the footsteps on the rooftop. Did Deniz see her? Theo listened for the mating dance of the *Panthera pardus ciscaucasica*. Theo mouthing the words now from his kid's encyclopedia open to L on the floor. Pan-the-ra. Par-dis. Kiss-cock-ass-sick-a. Reveling in the sexy Latin trinomial.

The female leopard circled in her cage. It was an oversized cage. Perfect cage for two lovers. He looked at the TV. He could not fathom the events unfolding on top of him. They were teasing Deniz. She was a beautiful specimen. That saxophone colour fur. Her name was Dunya. The cameras trained on the male. Would he pounce? Slaughter the trainer who likes to watch and ravage Dunya right there in the wet street? Deniz was deliberate. He turned his back, walked up to the point of the roof and crossed down to the opposite side. Evidently, the two leopards had history. It was true. News said the zoo was mating the two for a while now.

On the split screen, Cindy was interviewing a woman whose job it was to arrange for the impregnation of big cats. The woman described the mating patterns of the leopard.

There is intense mating for five straight days. During this time, leopards can mate four times per hour. Theo added it up. 4 times/hour x 24 hours in a day = 96 times a day. 96 x 5 days = 480 times if they didn't sleep. The lady explained that the female leopard does not ovulate regularly. No need for those digital ovulation tests that Theo bought. He recalled that happy face appearing in the test window. Go inseminate your wife now. The female leopard begins estrus because of the penis of the male. The leopard penis is unlike most other mammal penises. It is barbed. When the male pulls out repeatedly, this hurts the female. But the more this happens, the more likely the female is to produce eggs. So the male, not the female, is responsible for triggering the egg. Most likely, the woman explained, Deniz is not interested in the female because he can sense that Dunya is pregnant. When she's expecting, she no longer serves a biological function. So, he's not attracted to her. Cindy asked how he knows she's pregnant. Her urine. There is a different perfume to her urine when an egg is present. So, if the male knows he can make the female produce an egg, why do they mate every fifteen minutes for five days? Simple. The male of the species, like Deniz, has weak sperm. So he has to keep mating to make sure she gets pregnant. Do we know if Dunya is having a male or female leopard? It's too soon to tell. We are hoping for a boy though.

Theo thought he was better positioned to reunite the couple than the trainers or sex therapist. He could hurl open the attic bedroom window, it was more than large enough, whistle to the leopards, and let them mate freely in his father's bedroom. They could make a home there. Have the baby. He would name the baby Adam for a boy and Liv for a girl. They could devour the placenta. Grow old.

They waited about a half hour longer, but Deniz stayed put. One of the guys barked his orders. They carted the female away in her cage. Off to seduce other marooned male leopards around the world. Two grey trucks came down the street. New men got out. They walked in different directions and disappeared into the buildings around Theo's house. One by one they reappeared on different rooftops. The men looked at Deniz through binoculars. After Deniz turned down the meat and pussy — the two lures for men — there was only one option left. To put a bullet in his beautiful, worthless skull. When the caged female was almost out of sight, Deniz went back to the peak of the roof.

THREE

Rooftop Leopard Rejects Female changed to Special Weather Alert. Back to the apocalyptic gossip. Bizarre weather continued today on the East Coast, as hundreds of dead crabs washed up on the shore. Scientists are still looking to identify the cause of death. A Hurricane Warning is in effect for the evening and overnight period. A flood belt is training over the outskirts of the city.

The worst of Hurricane Catalina is yet to come. Last time was just a taste. This was the real deal. They were hours away from an extreme event, TV said. Strengthen the shell of your home. They cut to an expert on barricading. The helicopters above his house that night looked like ships in the fog caught in the light of lighthouses. Theo went downstairs. There was a foot of water in the basement. He kicked his way into the cellar.

After the Day of Blood, the construction workers left many sheets of plywood in the alley. Thick ones. He pulled them through the back door at night and piled them in the basement. He imagined using them to make himself a bivouac when he finally got dragged out of his father's house. That or a raft. He pulled out the pieces of plywood now one by one. Hammer. Nails. He boarded up the little basement windows with the small pieces. Then he took the big stuff to the main floor. He bolted a piece of plywood to the front door. It was already sealed from the outside. Then he nailed a few 2x4s across it. Same with the back door. The food door. The front window was also taken care of, but he reinforced it with another sheet of plywood. Even though all the windows and doors on the main floor were covered up after the Day of Blood, Theo still reinforced them all. Blocked the kitchen window. Blocked the dining-room window that looked out to the backyard. The side door. Back upstairs he covered the little window in his boyhood bedroom. He pulled in the generator from the second-floor balcony of the other room without being seen. He turned the power off. He heard the TV go silent. Covered up the sliding door. Back downstairs again he slid the hutch in front of the boarded-up front door. He shoved the couch down the hall and wedged it against the back door. Room by room he piled furniture against the holes of his father's house. He even tipped a bookcase in front of the fireplace. He saved the attic bedroom window for last. Deniz's window. He leaned a thick piece of plywood against the wall directly beneath it. The last hole in the house. He put his hammer and a fistful of large nails down on the window ledge beside the photograph. Out of the narrow opening of the curtain, Theo looked up at the night sky.

FOUR

As a boy, he was desperate for a photograph. But his father was deliberate. There are no pictures of your mother. Why do you need a photograph? Look in the mirror. You look just like her. He did entertain the notion, when he was a little boy, and before the kids at school explained their third-grade understanding of the vagina, that perhaps he had no mother at all. What he couldn't understand was why can't I remember her. Theo thought that maybe he was just made out of a piece of his father. Like he learned in Sunday school about Eve being made out of Adam's rib. Or like in the book of myths, where Venus was born out of a part severed from a god thrown into the sea. He thought about his father's missing finger. The one that was cut off building the roof of the house. The one that made him quit playing with the Bones of Adam. He wondered what happened to that finger. Despite all the roofers clamouring desperately through the construction materials right after the accident, it was never found. It must still be somewhere in the house.

On the first letter he read from his mother to his father, there was no address. Just O. Vesta on the top right corner. Theo didn't understand the O. His father told him that her name was Liv. She was Liv in all the stories. Anyway, she's mom to you. What is Liv short for? It's just Liv. His father knew that it wasn't just Liv, but he also knew that she would never be found and that the boy should stop looking. Just another one of the Biblical nameless like the Hemorrhaging

Woman. But Theo looked for Liv. He took out a baby name book from the library which he never returned. Theo found Olliva, Ollivani, Oliviana, Olivetta, Olivianne, Olivia. He kept looking for clues in the few letters his father let him see. In one, she had written the return address as Saturnalia, California. She signed it I love you, Licinia. On another one she signed off as Rhea Silvia from Divalia, N.Y. Finally, after exhausting his bedroom globe, he learned, with the help of a stolen grade-six school world map with Stephanie on the inside cover, that these were indeed fake cities. This mom doesn't want to be found.

On the map he did find a town called Olivia and a town called Vesta. What's more, they were both in Minnesota. And they were only 40 miles apart. He found a Vesta, Virginia. Vestal, New York. There was a Vesta, Ontario. But it was a ghost town. Only thing left was the ruined bell tower of St. Michael's church. In the phone book, he found the last name Vestalia and Vestal, but no O. Vesta. No Liv Vesta.

He tried to track her down right before he married Catalina. There were a few would-be moms. Two women who had changed their names. One didn't open the door. The other, flattered to be a mystery mother, gave him rosehip tea and sent him on his way. But in the end, the trail went cold. He needed more to go on. His dad was no help. Theo wished he could bloodtrail his mom like a hind. Theo tried to imagine what they'd talk about if he did find her. She would tell him things for little boys. Comb your hair. Tuck in your shirt. She would ask if he was tired and come into his room with a glass of water before he fell asleep to read him a story or say bedtime prayers.

He imagined how they would meet. They would hug. She would be thin. Pretty. He would feel her again for the first time since he was born. When he only knew her from the inside. And his body would remember hers like a childhood sickness, like chicken pox at three years, now dormant in his body, preventing itself from ever returning in the exact way as it hurt him the first time. Seeing his mom would be a new hurt. In the end, Theo never found her. He just wanted her to know that he was still waiting. Theo felt that in her all lost things are found again.

FIVE

When Theo moved back in as his dad starting dying, his boyhood room reminded him of things that children know. Like names of extinct animals and planetary moons and midriffs of certain girls. Lying in his old bed, he remembered Hillary Montes.

Looking through the telescope was always time to think about girls. Theo got a telescope that he paid for in change when he was 10. It was Nick's. He told Nick that he got it for the same reason all boys do. To try to see a naked woman. He was sick of his naked eye. Nick, that little pervert, swore up and down about not just the tits he would see, but the pussy too. That meant the price went up. Or you can look at Uranus, you faggot.

On the first night with the telescope, Theo turned all the lights off. His father wasn't home. And wouldn't be. He scanned the buildings around him. The first body part he caught in a third-floor window filled the whole field of vision. Just flesh. But it was only a hand. Most he ever saw was a couple kissing. He touched himself thinking of Hillary Montes. Mostly he saw people not touching.

Theo knew that not only was Hillary Montes just a name in his encyclopedia, but it wasn't even an actual girl's name. It was the name of Pluto's moon. And the reason that he knew the name of Pluto's moon was because the real reason he smashed open the pig to buy the telescope wasn't because of naked women, it was because of his mom.

He looked up Vesta in the phone book and the map. But he also tried the pages of his children's encyclopedia. And he found her. There were two entries. The first. Vesta: virgin goddess of the home. The second, 4 Vesta: one of the biggest asteroids in the entire asteroid belt. The brightest asteroid that can be seen from earth.

Theo knew that the planets were named after the Greek gods, and that the Romans stole their gods and called them by different names. Kids always know the names of dead gods. Theo knew that planets had families too. Mars was the son of Jupiter. Jupiter the son of Saturn. Saturn the son of Uranus. He learned how to find some planets with his telescope, but once he knew where they were, he was amazed that he could sometimes see them with his naked eye. He thought there was something wrong with him at first. Like maybe he was a god. But he wasn't. Theo got to like using his naked eye. He looked for girls with his naked eye. He never found any, but he learned how to see Mercury, Venus, Mars, and Jupiter. He liked to look for Saturn best though because the book said it was the furthest planet that you can see with just your eyes.

He read about Saturn in his mythology book. It was the story of the creation of the world. Saturn's mother begged her son to hurt his own father Uranus, because he was a bad god. None of the other children were brave enough to do it. The book said that Saturn cut off part of his father's body. Then threw it into the sea. Then a girl came out of the sea. Venus. Theo liked to stare at the picture of Venus. You couldn't see anything, but still.

He loved the mythological creatures in the book. At school he made up creatures. He started by drawing a normal man, then giving him hooves instead of feet. Another guy had horns. He drew a girl with snakes for hair. Half bird, half woman. Head of a man, body of a bull, with wings. A whole family with human heads and snake bodies. A woman with a scorpion tail. Then just a human head with crab legs. He got sick of the human head ones. He made a girl with a lion's head and a boy with a bull's head. Then he moved onto humans with parts of more than one animal. He drew a man with an elephant's trunk and for his hands he drew the claws of an eagle. In his myth book he loved the stories of dogs and cats turning into people. Or the one with an animal peeling off his skin and marrying a woman. Gods in animal form. Women giving birth to babies that were half-animal and half-human.

When he was a kid, he ripped out a page of a magazine that said World's First Picture of a God. Below was a colour picture of the Cave of the Three Brothers in France. The cave paintings were done at least 12,000 years before Christ. One was called The Sorcerer. It was drawn in black charcoal. It had human eyes. Stag horns. Two legs. No mouth. Long beard. Praying hands. Tail. Penis pointing backwards. This was a picture of their god. On the left-hand side of god was Venus. The magazine said her vagina is the central element of the painting. Her vulva was opened with a sharp stone tool. Theo looked up vulva in his encyclopedia. Vulva was not listed. She is the only full woman drawn in the cave. Elsewhere are four images of vaginas without bodies. Beside Venus there are two cats.

Six

These days, before Hurricane Catalina tried to drown him and a leopard appeared on his roof, Theo was getting ready to look for Uranus. With luck he would see 4 Vesta too. He never managed to see her before. He didn't quite know what he was looking for. Just a tiny egg in the sky, he guessed.

The sun was going down on the crowd. It was wild out there. A mass hysteria party for the end of the world. People were passing bottles. Some crazy girl was doing a fire act. A few girls were playing guitar and singing. Some junkies doing a rain dance. The graffiti artist perfecting the cock on the wall again. Covering it with a giant fig leaf. Then roughing in the body of Adam around it. There were more Theo masks too. A guy shouting Leopard Man masks. Other people had black eyes drawn on with eyeliner or black magic marker. The photo of Theo was front page in all the newspapers. Everyone was trying to lay claim to Deniz. The zoo people. The cops. Animal rights activists. Apocalypse enthusiasts. Leaders of religious castrations cults. The leopard just wandered Theo's rooftop.

Theo came back to the slit in the curtain when the crowd started shrieking. It sounded like it was made up of all women's voices. The voice of every woman he ever knew. His mother's voice heard in utero. Then Catalina the runaway. Then the bleeding and lactating women of his dad's dementia porno. Then Dalila and the whores. At first he thought Deniz pounced and was ravaging the crowds. No. Deniz was standing on the corner of the roof looking at the sky. A black armoured vehicle pushed through the crowd. Men dressed in grey with black flak jackets and masks got out. This was a special group of men. They looked like celestial police. The negotiators failed. No one could talk Deniz down. Men disappeared into the building across the street again. Appeared on the roof. They cleared the people from the rooftops. The people came out into the street and merged with the crowd. Theo heard banging on his back door. He knew the cops couldn't get in. It would take them hours to get past the barricades. The only way in was the attic window. Theo stood up. For the first time, he pulled the curtains back and stuck his head out the window in full view of the crowds. The rain started up again, but no one wanted to move. Someone on the ground spotted him. Look, it's the Leopard Man. The crowd looked up. They started cheering and chanting. A huge spotlight made a white circle around Theo. He heard the beat of helicopter wings. Someone was screaming please Theo, please. It was a woman. But Theo didn't look down. Nor would he ever look down. Just like his father taught him the first time he brought him up on the rooftops. He stood up on the window ledge and held onto the roof. Don't look down, Theo. Theo looked at the city. Somewhere out there in the night was a lone female baboon. Genitals red and swollen. There on his own roof was a Persian leopard from the Turkish mountains whose name means sea. Deniz walked to Theo's side of the roof.

Hello, Deniz. A group of people below put their arms together to form a net under Theo's window thinking he was going to jump. The cops cut the floodlight. Theo watched the last sliver of sun disappear behind Deniz. He stared at the leopard. One woman gives birth to another, Theo thought. And the other gives birth to her own mother. Theo mouthed the words. Day and night.

He whistled to Deniz, but Deniz couldn't hear him over the crowd. The rain started in hard. Hurricane Catalina. Theo looked over his shoulder at the roof across the street. The cop lay down on the lip of the roof. Looked through his scope.

The Remington. Theo starting screaming Deniz. Nothing. He didn't move. Deniz. Look at me, Deniz. Look at me. A shirtless woman activist got back up onto the roof across the street and ran towards the cop. There was a gun shot. Deniz leapt right in front of the attic window like an old man cat. The crowd scattered screaming. Deniz was still standing. Theo checked for blood on the roof. No blood. Either a miss or hit to the balls. The cops wrestled the woman on the roof to the ground. Deniz. Theo screamed. Please. His voice lost in Hurricane Catalina. The leopard didn't move. He was going to die up there on the roof. Theo jumped inside. He rushed to the bed and put his head to the floor. Theo pushed aside the little white bowl. Picked up his father's saxophone. Looked at the egg-shaped picture on the windowsill. It was the photo found inside the crown of his dead dad's teardrop fedora. Theo and his mom on his second birthday. On the back of the photo in black pen it said the day baby Theo finally got his sight. His dad never told him. Theo was born blind. For an instant he pictured his mom discovering after six months that her baby boy couldn't see. Understanding why he never smiled back at her. Why he stared into the sky and sobbed and thrashed against the bars in the corner of his dark crib. He let the photo slip out the window.

He put the sax to his lips and did the only thing he knew how. The only thing his father ever taught him. He screamed into the mouthpiece. Spitting and snarling. The female growl. Deniz turned his head. For the first time, the two looked at each other. Down on the ground men were shouting commands. The cops were pushing back the crowds who were trying to rush the house. Break the doors down. Theo knew they wouldn't get in. He looked at the cop on the roof. He growled once more on the sax. Screaming as loud as he could with his mouth closed. Then Theo stood aside. Deniz took a few small steps forward, then leapt through the open window into the bedroom and up onto the king bed of Theo's dead father. He took the saxophone out of his mouth. Put a nail between his teeth. Theo breathed in. The leopard smelled like orange blossoms. He took the last piece of plywood, placed it carefully over the window, and nailed it shut.

OTHER RECENT QUATTRO FICTION

Rough Paradise by Alec Butler
Look at Me by Robert Shoub
Dempsey's Lodge by Eric Wright
Inheritance by Kirsten Gundlack
Oatcakes and Courage by Joyce Grant-Smith
Terminal Grill by Rosemary Aubert
World of Glass by Jocelyne Dubois
The Sandbar by Jean-Paul Daoust
Texas by Claudio Gaudio
Abundance of the Infinite by Christopher Canniff
The Proxy Bride by Terri Favro
Tea with the Tiger by Nathan Unsworth
A Certain Grace by Binnie Brennan
Life Without by Ken Klonsky
Romancing the Buzzard by Leah Murray
The Lebanese Dishwasher by Sonia Saikaley
Against God by Patrick Senécal
The Ballad of Martin B. by Michael Mirolla
Mahler's Lament by Deborah Kirshner